Recipient of the prestigious Mystery Writers of America Grand Master award and author of novels that range from noir to thriller to everything in between, Donald E. Westlake has compiled an unrivaled literary oeuvre. This story introduced John Dortmunder to the world, started an acclaimed series, became a classic movie starring Robert Redford, and launched a literary genre of its own: the comic crime caper.

THE HOT ROCK

John Dortmunder left prison with the warm words of the warden ringing in his ears and not one chance of going straight. Soon Dortmunder was riding in a stolen Cadillac with venetian blinds, reuniting with old friends and scheming to heist a large emerald belonging to a small African nation. As always, his planning is meticulous. As always, the execution is not. Undaunted, Dortmunder is now chasing the gem by plane, train, and automobile. Because this hot rock has a way of getting stolen—not just once, but again and again and again . . .

"WESTLAKE'S NOVEL COMES AWESOMELY CLOSE TO THE ULTIMATE IN COMIC, BIG-CAPER NOVELS; IT'S SO FILLED WITH . . . ACTION AND IMAGINATION."

—*New York Times Book Review*

"WESTLAKE IS A MASTER HAND AT THE RUNNING GAG. . . . THIS WESTLAKE BROUGHT ON SUCH A CASE OF THE LAUGHING BENDS THAT I REQUIRED DECOMPRESSION."

—*Washington Post*

BY DONALD E. WESTLAKE

NOVELS
The Hook • The Ax • Humans • Sacred Monster • A Likely Story • Kahawa • Brothers Keepers • I Gave at the Office Adios, Scheherazade • Up Your Banners

THE DORTMUNDER SERIES
Bad News
What's the Worst That Could Happen? • Don't Ask
Drowned Hopes • Good Behavior
Why Me • Nobody's Perfect
Jimmy the Kid • Bank Shot • The Hot Rock

COMIC CRIME NOVELS
Smoke • Baby, Would I Lie? • Trust Me on This • High Adventure • Castle in the Air • Enough • Dancing Aztecs Two Much • *Help* I Am Being Held Prisoner Cops and Robbers • Somebody Owes Me Money Who Stole Sassi Manoon? • God Save the Mark The Spy in the Ointment • The Busy Body The Fugitive Pigeon

CRIME NOVELS
Pity Him Afterwards • Killy • 361
Killing Time • The Mercenaries

JUVENILE
Philip

WESTERN
Gangway (with Brian Garfield)

REPORTAGE
Under an English Heaven

SHORT STORIES
Tomorrow's Crimes • Levine
The Curious Facts Preceding My Execution
and Other Fictions • A Good Story and Other Stories

ANTHOLOGY
Once Against the Law (coedited with William Tenn)

DONALD E. WESTLAKE

THE
HOT ROCK

THE FIRST DORTMUNDER NOVEL

Published by Warner Books

A Time Warner Company

Copyright © 1970 by Donald E. Westlake
Copyright © renewed 1998 by Donald E. Westlake
All rights reserved. No part of this publication may be reproduced or transmitted in any form or by any means, electronic or mechanical, including photocopy, recording, or any information storage and retrieval system, without permission in writing from the publisher.

Cover illustration by Sonja Lamut and Nenad Jakesevic

 Mysterious Press books are published by Warner Books, Inc.,
1271 Avenue of the Americas, New York, NY 10020.

Visit our Web site at www.twbookmark.com

A Time Warner Company

The Mysterious Press name and logo are registered trademarks of Warner Books, Inc.

First Trade Printing: April 2001

10 9 8 7 6 5 4 3

Library of Congress Cataloging-in-Publication Data

Westlake, Donald E.
    The hot rock / Donald E. Westlake.
        p. cm.
    ISBN 0-446-67703-5
    1. Dortmunder (Fictitious character)—Fiction.   2. Criminals—Fiction.   I. Title.

PS3573.E9 H68 2001
813'.54—dc21

00-053414

This is for Milt Amgott,
who has helped to keep me from a life of crime
by making it superfluous.

The criminal is the type of the strong man in unfavorable surroundings, the strong man made sick.
—F. W. NIETZSCHE

MEETING JOHN

One day in 1967 I was wearing my Richard Stark hat, looking for a story to tell about my man Parker, and I thought, he reacts badly to frustration, what if he had to steal the same thing four or five times? I started to work it out, then realized the idea was only comic and Parker wouldn't stand for it. But I still liked the notion, and even—once it was comic—saw how to make it *six* thefts of the same elusive item. So I'd do it that way.

But if it wasn't Parker, who was it? Who was this guy, dogged but doomed, and what was his name? Without a name, I couldn't see him, and until I could see him I couldn't write about him.

For a long time I just couldn't think of the right name, and then one day, I was in a bar—the only time in my life—and one of the neon beer logos on the back-bar said "DAB—Dortmunder Actien Bier," and I said, "That's what I want, an action hero with something wrong with him," and John Dortmunder was born.

Almost. I started the book, and went along happily for a while, but after three heists I just ran out of steam, decided it wasn't such a good idea after all, and put the half-novel away forever.

But then, two years later, we were doing some remodeling, and I had to clean out a closet, and came across the partial manuscript, which I had more or less forgotten about. (Why remember failures?) So I sat down and read it, and enjoyed it, and suddenly it stopped. I had to finish the book to find out what happened next.

So there it was, finally complete. Having realized *The Habitual Crime* wasn't a good title after all, I renamed it THE HOT ROCK, and John Dortmunder's one and only story was ready to fly.

—Donald E. Westlake

Editor's Note—The John Dortmunder series (to date):

THE HOT ROCK

PHASE ONE

1

Dortmunder blew his nose. "Warden," he said, "you don't know how much I appreciate the personal attention you been paying me." There wasn't anything for him to do with the Kleenex, so he just held it balled up in his fist.

Warden Outes gave him a brisk smile, got up from behind his desk, walked around to Dortmunder's side, patted him on the arm, and said, "It's the ones I can save that give me the most pleasure." He was a latter-day Civil Service type—college-trained, athletic, energetic, reformistic, idealistic, and chummy. Dortmunder hated him.

The warden said, "I'll walk you to the gate, Dortmunder."

"You don't have to do that, Warden," Dortmunder said. The Kleenex was cold and gooey against his palm.

"But it will give me pleasure," the warden said. "To see you walk out that gate, and know you'll never slip again, you'll never be inside these walls again, and to know I had some small part in your rehabilitation, you can't imagine how much pleasure that will give me."

Dortmunder was feeling no pleasure at all. He'd sold his cell for three hundred bucks—having a hot water faucet that worked and a tunnel to the dispensary made it a bargain at the price—and the money was supposed to be passed to him on his way out. He couldn't have taken it before then or it would have been found in the final shakedown. But how could it be delivered with the warden standing right next to him?

He said, playing a little desperation ball, "Warden, it's in this office that I've always seen you, in this office that I've listened to your—"

"Come along, Dortmunder," the warden said. "We can talk on our way to the gate."

So they went to the gate together. On the last lap, crossing the big yard, Dortmunder saw Creasey, the trusty with the three C's, start in his direction and then abruptly stop. Creasey made a small gesture that meant, There's nothing to be done.

Dortmunder made a small gesture that meant, God damn it to hell, I *know* there's nothing to be done.

At the gate, the warden stuck his hand out and said, "Good luck, Dortmunder. May I say I hope I never see you again." It was a joke, because he chuckled.

Dortmunder switched the Kleenex to his left hand. It was really full, it had seeped all over his palm. He took the warden's hand and said, "I hope I never see you again either, Warden." It wasn't a joke, but he chuckled anyway.

The warden's expression had suddenly become a bit glassy. "Yes," he said. "Yes."

Dortmunder turned away, and the warden looked down at his palm.

The big gate opened, Dortmunder stepped outside, the big gate closed. He was free, his debt to society was paid. He was also out three hundred fish, God damn it. He'd been counting on that dough. All he had was ten bucks and a train ticket.

Disgusted, he threw the Kleenex on the sidewalk.

Littering.

2

Kelp saw Dortmunder walk out into the sunlight and then just stand there a minute,
looking around. Kelp knew what that feeling was, the
first minute of freedom, free air, free sun. He waited,
not wanting to spoil Dortmunder's pleasure, but when
Dortmunder finally started to walk off along the sidewalk, Kelp started the engine and steered the long black
car slowly down the street after him.

It was a pretty good car, a Cadillac with side curtains, Venetian blinds across the back window, air conditioning, a gizmo that would keep the car moving at
any desired speed without having your foot on the gas,
a gizmo that would switch down your high beams at
night when another car was coming, all sorts of labor-
saving devices. Kelp had picked it up last night down
in New York. He'd preferred to drive up here today rather
than take the train, so he'd gone shopping for a car last
night, and he'd found this one on East 67th Street. It
had MD plates and he always automatically checked

those, because doctors tend to leave the keys in the car, and once again the medical profession had not disappointed him.

It didn't have MD plates now, of course. The state hadn't spent four years teaching him how to make license plates for nothing.

He glided along after Dortmunder now, the long black Caddy purring along, tires crunching the dirty pavement, and Kelp thought how surprised and pleased Dortmunder would be to see a friendly face the first thing on hitting the street. He was just about to hit the horn when Dortmunder suddenly spun around, looked at the silent black car with side curtains following him, got a panicky look on his face, and began to run like hell along the sidewalk, cowering against the gray prison wall.

There were four buttons on a control panel in the door, and they operated the four side windows of the Cadillac. The only trouble was, Kelp could never remember which button operated which window. He pushed a button and the right rear window slid down. "Dortmunder!" he shouted, hitting the accelerator, the Caddy leaping forward along the street. There was no one else in sight, only the black car and the running man. The prison wall loomed tall and gray, and across the street the small grimy houses were closed and silent, shades and drapes blinding their windows.

Kelp was veering all over the street, his attention distracted by his confusion over the window buttons. The left rear window rolled down, and he shouted Dortmunder's name again, but Dortmunder still couldn't hear him. His fingers found another button, pushed, and the right rear window rolled up again.

The Caddy jounced up over the curb, the tires slewed across the weedy space between curb and sidewalk, and then Kelp's car was angling straight for Dortmunder, who turned, flattened his back against the wall, spread his arms out wide to both sides, and screamed like a banshee.

At the last second, Kelp hit the brakes. They were power brakes, and he hit them hard, and the Caddy stopped dead, bouncing Kelp off the steering wheel.

Dortmunder reached one shaky hand out and leaned on the Caddy's quivering hood.

Kelp tried to get out of the car, but in his excitement he'd hit another button, the one that automatically locked all four doors. "Damn doctors!" Kelp cried, pushed every button in sight, and finally lunged from the car like a skin diver escaping from an octopus.

Dortmunder was still standing against the wall, leaning forward slightly, supporting himself with one hand on the car hood. He looked gray, and it wasn't all prison pallor.

Kelp walked over to him. "What are you running for, Dortmunder?" he said. "It's me, your old pal, Kelp." He stuck his hand out.

Dortmunder hit him in the eye.

3

All you had to do was honk," Dortmunder said. He was grousing because his knuckle was stinging where he'd skinned it on Kelp's cheekbone. He put the knuckle in his mouth.

"I was going to," Kelp said, "but things got kind of confused. But they're okay now?"

They were on the express road to New York, the Caddy's speed set at sixty-five miles an hour. Kelp had to keep one hand on the wheel and occasionally glance out front to see they were still on the road, but other than that the car was driving itself.

Dortmunder was feeling aggrieved. Three hundred bucks down the drain, scared out of his wits, almost run down by a damn fool in a Cadillac, and skinned his knuckle, all on the same day. "What do you want, anyway?" he said. "They give me a train ticket, I didn't need no ride."

"You need work, I bet," Kelp said. "Unless you got something lined up."

"I don't have anything lined up," Dortmunder said. Now that he thought about it, that irritated him too.

"Well, I got a sweetheart for you," Kelp said. He was smiling all over his face.

Dortmunder decided to stop grousing. "All right," he said. "I can listen. What's the story?"

Kelp said, "Did you ever hear of a place called Talabwo?"

Dortmunder frowned. "Isn't that one of those South Pacific islands?"

"Naw, it's a country. In Africa."

"I never heard of it," Dortmunder said. "I heard of the Congo."

"This is near there," Kelp said. "I think it is."

"Those countries are all too hot, aren't they? I mean temperature hot."

"Yeah, I guess they are," Kelp said. "I don't know, I never been."

"I don't think I'd want to go there," Dortmunder said. "They got disease too. And they kill white people a lot."

"Just nuns," Kelp said. "But the job isn't over there, it's right here in the good old USA."

"Oh." Dortmunder sucked his knuckle, then said, "Then why talk about this other place?"

"Talabwo."

"Yeah, Talabwo. Why talk about it?"

"I'll get to that," Kelp said. "You ever hear of Akinzi?"

"He's that doctor did that sex book," Dortmunder said. "I wanted to get it out of the library in stir, but they had a twelve-year waiting list. I put my name on, just in case I got turned down for parole, but I never got the book. He's dead, isn't he?"

"That's not what I'm talking about," Kelp said. There was a truck moseying along in his lane, so Kelp had to do some driving for a minute. He steered into the other lane, went by the truck, and got back into his own lane again. Then he looked at Dortmunder and said, "I'm talking about a country. Another country. It's called Akinzi." He spelled it.

Dortmunder shook his head. "Is that in Africa too?"

"Oh, you heard of that one."

"No, I didn't," Dortmunder said. "I just guessed."

"Oh." Kelp glanced at the highway. "Yeah, it's another country in Africa," he said. "There was this British colony there, and when it went independent there was trouble, because there were two big tribes in the country and they both wanted to run it, so they had a civil war and finally they decided to split into two countries. So that's the two countries, Talabwo and Akinzi."

"You know an awful lot about this stuff," Dortmunder said.

"I got told about it," Kelp said.

Dortmunder said, "But I don't see any caper in it yet."

"I'm coming to that," Kelp said. "It seems that one of these tribes had this emerald, this jewel, and they used to pray to it like a god, and these days it's their symbol. Like a mascot. Like the tomb of the unknown soldier, something like that."

"An emerald?"

"It's supposed to be worth half a million bucks," Kelp said.

"That's a lot," Dortmunder said.

"Of course," Kelp said, "you couldn't fence a thing like that, it's too well known. And it would cost too much."

Dortmunder nodded. "I already thought of that," he said. "When I thought what you were going to say was heist the emerald."

"But that is what I'm going to say," Kelp said. "That's the caper, to heist the emerald."

Dortmunder found himself getting irritable again. He took his pack of Camels out of his shirt pocket. "If we can't fence it," he said, "what the hell do we want to lift it for?"

"Because we've got a buyer," Kelp said. "He'll pay thirty thousand dollars a man to get the emerald."

Dortmunder stuck a cigarette in his mouth and the pack in his pocket. "How many men?"

"We figure maybe five."

"That's a hundred fifty grand for a half-million-dollar stone. He's getting a bargain."

"We're getting thirty grand each," Kelp pointed out.

Dortmunder pushed in the cigarette lighter on the dashboard. "Who is this guy?" he said. "Some collector?"

"No. He's the UN Ambassador from Talabwo."

Dortmunder looked at Kelp. "He's who?"

The cigarette lighter popped out of the dashboard and fell on the floor.

Kelp repeated himself.

Dortmunder picked up the cigarette lighter and lit his cigarette. "Explain," he said.

"Sure," Kelp said. "When the British colony split into two countries, Akinzi got the city where the emerald was being kept. But Talabwo is the country where the tribe is that always had the emerald. The UN sent in some people to referee the situation, and Akinzi paid some money for the emerald, but money isn't the point. Talabwo wants the emerald."

Dortmunder shook the cigarette lighter and flipped it out the window. He said, "Why don't they go to war?"

"The two countries are even Stephen. They're a pair of welterweights, they'd ruin each other and nobody'd win."

Dortmunder dragged on the cigarette, exhaled through his nose. "If we cop the emerald and give it to Talabwo," he said, "why won't Akinzi go to the UN and say, 'Make them give us back our emerald'?" He sneezed.

"Talabwo won't let on they got it," Kelp said. "They don't want to display it or anything, they just want to have it. It's symbolic with them. Like those Scotchmen that stole the Stone of Scone a few years ago."

"The one that did what?"

"It's a thing that happened in England," Kelp said. "Anyway, about this emerald heist. You interested?"

"Depends," Dortmunder said. "Where's the emerald kept at?"

"Right now," Kelp said, "it's in the Coliseum in New York. There's this Pan-African display, all sorts of stuff from Africa, and the emerald's part of the display from Akinzi."

"So we're supposed to swipe it from the Coliseum?"

"Not necessarily," Kelp said. "The display's going on tour in a couple weeks. It'll be in a lot of different places, and it'll travel by train and truck. We'll get plenty of chances to get our hands on it."

Dortmunder nodded. "All right," he said. "We cop the emerald, we turn it over to this guy—"

"Iko," Kelp said, pronouncing it *eye-ko,* accent on the first syllable.

Dortmunder frowned. "Isn't that a Japanese camera?"

"No, it's the name of the UN Ambassador from Talabwo. And if you're interested in the job, that's who we're going to go see."

Dortmunder said, "He knows I'm coming?"

"Sure," Kelp said. "I told him what we needed was an organizer, a planner, and I told him Dortmunder was the best organizer in the business and if we were lucky we could get you to set things up for us. I didn't tell him you were just finishing a stretch."

"Good," Dortmunder said.

4

Major Patrick Iko, stocky, black, mustached, studied the dossier he'd been given on John Archibald Dortmunder and shook his head in amused contempt. He could understand why Kelp hadn't wanted to tell him that Dortmunder was just finishing a prison term, one of his famous plans having failed to go precisely to blueprint, but hadn't Kelp realized the Major would automatically look into the background of each of the men under consideration? He naturally had to be extremely selective about the men to whom he would entrust the Balabomo Emerald. He couldn't take a chance on picking some dishonest types who, having rescued the emerald from the Akinzi, would then steal it for themselves.

The great mahogany door opened and the Major's secretary, a slender, discreet ebony young man whose spectacles reflected the light, came in and said, "Sir, two gentlemen to see you. Mr. Kelp and another man."

"Show them in."

"Yes, sir." The secretary backed out.

The Major closed the dossier and put it away in a desk drawer. He then got to his feet and smiled with bland geniality at the two white men walking toward him across the great expanse of Oriental rug. "Mr. Kelp," he said. "How good to see you again."

"Nice to see you too, Major Iko," Kelp said. "This here is John Dortmunder, the fellow I told you about."

"Mr. Dortmunder." The Major bowed slightly. "Won't you both be seated?"

They all sat down, and the Major studied this man Dortmunder. It was always fascinating to see a man in the flesh after having known him only as a dossier, words typed on sheets of paper in a manila folder, photostats of documents, newspaper clippings, photos. Here was the man that dossier had attempted to describe. How close had it come?

In terms of facts, Major Iko knew quite a bit about John Archibald Dortmunder. He knew that Dortmunder was thirty-seven years of age, that he had been born in a small town in central Illinois, that he had grown up in an orphanage, that he had served in the United States Army in Korea during the police action there but had been on the other side of the cops-and-robbers game ever since, and that he had twice been in prison for robbery, the second term having ended with a parole just this morning. He knew that Dortmunder had been arrested several other times in robbery investigations, but that none of those other arrests had stuck. He knew that Dortmunder had never been arrested for any other crime, and that there didn't even appear to be any rumors concerning any murders, arsons, rapes, or kidnappings that he might have performed. And he knew that Dortmunder had been married in San Diego in 1952 to a night-club entertainer named Honeybun Bazoom, from whom he had won an uncontested divorce in 1954.

What did the man himself show? He was sitting now in the direct sunlight streaming in the park-view windows, and what he looked mostly like was a convalescent. A little gray, a little tired, face a little lined, thin body rather frail-looking. His suit was obviously new and obviously the cheapest quality made. His shoes were obviously old but had obviously cost quite a bit when new. The clothing indicated a man who had been used to living well but for whom times had recently turned bad. Dortmunder's eyes, as they met the Major's, were flat, watchful, unexpressive. A man who would keep his own counsel, the Major thought, and a man who would make his decisions slowly and then stand by them.

And stand by his word? The Major thought it worth taking the chance. He said, "Welcome back to the world, Mr. Dortmunder. I imagine freedom feels sweet right now."

Dortmunder and Kelp looked at each other.

The Major smiled and said, "Mr. Kelp didn't tell me."

"I know," Dortmunder said. "You been checking up on me."

"Naturally," the Major said. "Wouldn't you, in my position?"

"Maybe I ought to check up on you," Dortmunder said.

"Perhaps you should," the Major said. "They'd be happy to tell you about me at the UN. Or call your own State Department, I'm sure they have a file on me over there."

Dortmunder shrugged. "It doesn't matter. What did you find out about me?"

"That I can probably take a chance on you. Mr. Kelp tells me you make good plans."

"I try to."

"What happened the last time?"

"Something went wrong," Dortmunder said.

Kelp, rushing to his friend's defense, said, "Major, it wasn't his fault, it was just rotten luck. He had it figured for—"

"I've read the report," the Major told him. "Thank you." To Dortmunder he said, "It was a good plan, and you did run into bad luck, but I'm pleased to see you don't waste time justifying yourself."

"I can't play it over again," Dortmunder said. "Let's talk about this emerald of yours."

"Let's. Can you get it?"

"I don't know. How much help can you give us?"

The Major frowned. "Help? What kind of help?"

"We'll probably need guns. Maybe a car or two, maybe a truck, depending on how the job works up. We might need some other stuff."

"Oh, yes," the Major said. "I could supply any material you might need, certainly."

"Good." Dortmunder nodded and pulled a crumpled pack of Camels from his pocket. He lit a cigarette and leaned forward to drop the match in the ashtray on the

Major's desk. "About money," he said. "Kelp tells me it's thirty gee a man."

"Thirty thousand dollars, yes."

"No matter how many men?"

"Well," the Major said, "there should be some sort of limit on it. I wouldn't want you enlisting an army."

"What's the limit?"

"Mr. Kelp spoke of five men."

"All right. That's a hundred fifty gee. What if we do it with less men?"

"It would still be thirty thousand dollars a man."

Dortmunder said, "Why?"

"I wouldn't want to encourage you," the Major said, "to attempt the robbery with too few men. So it will be thirty thousand per man no matter how many or how few men are involved."

"Up to five."

"If you tell me six are absolutely necessary, I will pay for six."

Dortmunder nodded. He said, "Plus expenses."

"I beg your pardon?"

"This is going to be a full-time job for maybe a month, maybe six weeks," Dortmunder said. "We need money to live on."

"You mean you want an advance on the thirty thousand."

"No. I mean I want expense money over and above the thirty thousand."

The Major shook his head. "No, no," he said. "I'm sorry, that wasn't the agreement. Thirty thousand dollars a man, and that's all."

Dortmunder got to his feet and stubbed out the Camel in the Major's ashtray. It smoldered. Dortmunder said, "See you around," and, "Come on, Kelp," and started for the door.

The Major couldn't believe it. He called, "Are you going?"

Dortmunder turned at the door and looked at him. "Yeah."

"But why?"

"You're too cheap. You'd make me nervous to work for you. I'd come to you for a gun, you wouldn't want to give me more than one bullet." Dortmunder reached for the doorknob.

The Major said, "Wait."

Dortmunder waited, hand on knob.

The Major thought fast, adding up budgets. "I'll give you one hundred dollars a week per man living expenses," he said.

"Two hundred," Dortmunder said. "Nobody can live in New York City on one hundred a week."

"One-fifty," the Major said.

Dortmunder hesitated, and the Major could see him trying to decide whether or not to hold out for the full amount.

Kelp, who'd just been sitting there all this time, said, "That's a fair price, Dortmunder. What the hell, it's only for a few weeks."

Dortmunder shrugged and took his hand off the knob. "All right," he said. He came back and sat down. "What can you tell me about how this emerald's guarded and where it's kept?"

A wavering thin ribbon of smoke extended up from the smoldering Camel, as though tiny Cherokees had set up a campfire in the ashtray. The line was directly between the Major and Dortmunder, making him feel cross-eyed when he tried to focus on Dortmunder's face. But he was too proud either to stub out the cigarette or move his head, so he squinted one eye half shut and went on to answer Dortmunder's questions:

"All I know is, the Akinzi have it very well guarded. I've tried to learn the details, how many guards and so on, but they are being kept secret."

"But it's in the Coliseum now."

"Yes. Part of the Akinzi exhibit."

"All right. We'll go take a look at it. Where do we get our money?"

The Major looked blank. "Your money?"

"This week's hundred fifty."

"Oh." It was all happening a little too fast. "I'll call our finance office downstairs. You can stop in there on your way out."

"Good." Dortmunder got to his feet, and a second later so did Kelp. Dortmunder said, "I'll get in touch with you if I need anything."

The Major was sure of that.

5

"D oesn't look much like half a million bucks to me," Dortmunder said.

"Just so it's thirty thousand," Kelp said. "Each."

The emerald, many-faceted, deeply green, a little smaller than a golf ball, nested in a small white trivet on a cloth of red satin on a table completely enclosed in glass, all four sides and the top. The glass cube was about six feet square and seven feet high, and at a distance of about five feet out from it a red velvet rope looped from stanchions to make a larger square to keep the gawkers at a safe distance. At each corner of this larger square, just inside the rope, stood a colored guard in a dark blue uniform with a holstered gun on his hip. A small sign on a one-legged stand like a music stand said BALABOMO EMERALD in capital letters and gave the stone's history, the dates and names and places.

Dortmunder studied the guards. They looked bored, but not sleepy. He studied the glass, and it had the slightly olive look of glass with a lot of metal in it. Bulletproof, shatterproof, burglarproof. The edges of the glass cube were lined with strips of chromed steel and so was the line where the glass met the floor.

They were on the second floor of the Coliseum, the ceiling about thirty feet above their heads, a balcony overlooking the floor on three sides. The Pan-African Culture and Art Exhibit was spread throughout all four display floors, with the main attractions here on the second floor. The high ceiling bounced back a general stirring of sound as people shuffled by the exhibits.

Akinzi not being a very large or important African nation, it wasn't out in the very middle of the floor, but the Balabomo Emerald being considered an impressive stone, it wasn't shoved back against a wall or up onto the fourth floor either. It stood in a fairly exposed position, miles from any exit.

"I've seen enough," Dortmunder said.

"Me too," said Kelp.

They left the Coliseum and went across Columbus Circle and into Central Park. They took a path that headed for the lake and Dortmunder said, "That would be tough, taking it out of there."

"Yeah, it would," said Kelp.

"I wonder maybe we should wait till it goes on the road," Dortmunder said.

"That won't be for a while yet," said Kelp. "Iko won't like us sitting around doing nothing at a hundred fifty bucks a week per man."

"Forget Iko," Dortmunder said. "If we do this thing, I'm the one in charge. I'll handle Iko, don't worry about it."

"Sure, Dortmunder," said Kelp. "Anything you say."

They walked on over to the lake and sat on a bench there. It was June and Kelp watched the girls walk by. Dortmunder sat looking at the lake.

He didn't know about this caper, he didn't know whether he liked it or not. He liked the idea of the guaranteed return, and he liked the idea of the small easily transported object of the heist, and he was pretty sure he could keep Iko from causing any trouble, but on the other hand he had to be careful. He'd fallen twice now, it wouldn't be a good thing to fall again. He didn't want to spend the rest of his life eating prison food.

So what didn't he like? Well, for one thing, they were going after an item valued at half a million dollars, and it only stood to reason an item valued at half a million dollars was going to get some pretty heavy guarding. It wasn't going to be easy to get that rock away from the Akinzi. The four guards, the bulletproof glass, that was probably only the beginning of the defenses.

For another thing, if they did manage to get away with the stone, they could count on very heavy police activity. The cops would be likely to spend considerably more time and energy tracking down the people who stole a half-million-dollar emerald than going after somebody who copped a portable television set. There would also be insurance dicks all over the place, and sometimes they were worse than the cops.

And finally, how did he know Iko could be trusted? There was something just a little too smooth about that bird.

He said, "What do you think of Iko?"

Kelp, surprised, looked away from the girl in the green stockings and said, "He's okay, I guess. Why?"

"You think he'll pay up?"

Kelp laughed. "Sure he'll pay up," he said. "He wants the emerald, he *has* to pay up."

"What if he doesn't? We wouldn't find any buyer anywhere else."

"Insurance company," Kelp said promptly. "They'd pay a hundred fifty gee for a half-million-dollar rock any day."

Dortmunder nodded. "Maybe," he said, "that would be the better system anyway."

Kelp didn't get it. "What would?" he said.

"We let Iko finance the job," Dortmunder said. "But when we get the emerald we sell it to the insurance company instead."

"I don't like that," Kelp said.

"Why not?"

"Because he knows who we are," Kelp said, "and if this emerald is this big symbolic thing for the people in his country, they could get awful upset if we cop it for ourselves, and I don't want some whole African country out to get me, money or no money."

"Okay," Dortmunder said. "Okay. We'll see how it plays."

"A whole country out to get me," Kelp said and shivered. "I wouldn't like that."

"All right."

"Blow guns and poison arrows," Kelp said and shivered again.

"I think they're more modern now," Dortmunder said.

Kelp looked at him. "Is that supposed to make me feel better? Tommy guns and airplanes."

"All right," Dortmunder said. "All right." To change the subject, he said, "Who do you think we should bring in with us?"

"The rest of the team?" Kelp shrugged. "I dunno. What kind of guys do we need?"

"It's hard to say." Dortmunder frowned at the lake, ignoring a girl going by in a tiger-stripe leotard. "No specialists," he said, "except maybe a lockman. But nobody for safes, nothing like that."

"We want five or six?"

"Five," Dortmunder said. He announced one of the rules he lived by: "If you can't do a job with five men, you can't do it at all."

"Okay," said Kelp. "So we'll want a driver, and a lockman, and a utility outfielder."

"Right," said Dortmunder. "For the lockman, there was that little guy in Des Moines. You know the one I mean?"

"Something like Wise? Wiseman? Welsh?"

"Whistler!" said Dortmunder.

"That's it!" said Kelp and shook his head. "He's in stir. They got him for letting a lion loose."

Dortmunder turned his head away from the lake and looked at Kelp. "They did what?"

Kelp shrugged. "Don't blame me," he said. "That's just what I heard. He took his kids to the zoo, he got bored, he started to play around with the locks kind of absentminded, like you or me might doodle, and the first thing you know he let a lion loose."

"That's nice," Dortmunder said.

"Don't blame me," Kelp said. Then he said, "What about Chefwick? You know him?"

"The railroad nut. He's crazy out of his head."

"But he's a great lockman," Kelp said. "And he's available."

"Okay," Dortmunder said. "Give him a call."

"I will." Kelp watched two girls in various shades of green and gold go by. "Now we need a driver," he said.

"How about Lartz? Remember him?"

"Forget him," Kelp said. "He's in the hospital."

"Since when?"

"A couple weeks ago. He ran into a plane."

Dortmunder gave him a long slow look. "He did what?"

"It ain't my fault," Kelp said. "The way I heard it, he was at the wedding of some cousin of his out on the Island, he was coming back into town, he took the Van Wyck Expressway the wrong way by mistake, the first thing he knew he was out to Kennedy Airport. He was a little drunk, I guess, and—"

"Yeah," Dortmunder said.

"Yeah. And he got confused by the signs, and he wound up on taxiway seventeen and he ran into this Eastern Airlines plane that just come up from Miami."

"Taxiway seventeen," Dortmunder said.

"That's what I heard," Kelp said.

Dortmunder pulled out his Camels and stuck one

thoughtfully in his face. He offered the pack to Kelp, but Kelp shook his head and said, "I gave them up. Those cancer commercials got to me."

Dortmunder paused with the cigarettes held out in mid-air. He said, "Cancer commercials."

"Sure. On television."

"I haven't seen any television in four years," Dortmunder said.

"You missed something," Kelp said.

"Apparently I did," Dortmunder said. "Cancer commercials."

"That's right. Scare the life out of you. Wait till you see one."

"Yeah," Dortmunder said. He put the pack away and lit the cigarette in his face. "About a driver," he said. "Did you hear about anything odd happening to Stan Murch lately?"

"Stan? No. What happened?"

Dortmunder looked at him again. "I was asking you."

Kelp shrugged in bewilderment. "Last I heard he was fine," he said.

"Then why don't we use him," Dortmunder said.

"If you're sure he's okay," Kelp said.

Dortmunder sighed. "I'll call him and ask," he said.

"Now," Kelp said. "About our utility outfielder."

"I'm afraid to mention anybody," Dortmunder said.

Kelp looked at him in surprise. "Why? You got good judgment."

Dortmunder sighed. "How about Ernie Danforth?" he said.

Kelp shook his head. "He quit the racket," he said.

"He quit?"

"Yeah. He become a priest. See, the way I heard it, he was watching this Pat O'Brien movie on the Late—"

"All *right*." Dortmunder got to his feet. He snapped his cigarette into the lake. "I want to know about Alan Greenwood," he said, his voice tight, "and all I want is a yes or a no."

Kelp was bewildered again. Blinking up at Dortmunder, he said, "A yes or a no what?"

"Can we use him!"

An old lady, who had been glowering at Dortmunder since he'd thrown his cigarette into the lake, suddenly blanched and hurried away.

Kelp said, "Sure we can use him. Why not? Greenwood's a good man."

"I'll call him!" Dortmunder shouted.

"I can hear you," Kelp said. "I can hear you."

Dortmunder looked around. "Let's go get a drink," he said.

"Sure," Kelp said, jumping to his feet. "Anything you say. Sure. Sure."

6

They were on the straightaway now. "All right, baby," Stan Murch muttered through clenched teeth. "This is it."

He was hunched over the wheel, his fingers in their kid gloves clutching the wheel, his foot tense on the accelerator, his eyes flicking down to the instrument panel, reading the dials there, checking it all out: speedometer, odometer, tachometer, fuel gauge, temperature, oil pressure, clock. He strained against the chest harness holding him against the seat, willing his car forward, seeing the long sleek nose come closer and closer to the guy in front of him. He was going to pass on the inside, by the rail, and once past this one it would be clear sailing.

But now the other guy was aware of him closing the gap, and Murch sensed the other car pulling away, keeping ahead of the danger.

No. It wasn't going to happen. Murch checked the rearview mirror, and everything was all right back there.

He tromped down on the accelerator, the Mustang went into overdrive, he shot on by the green Pontiac, he angled across two lanes and let his foot ease on the accelerator. The Pontiac roared by on his left, but Murch didn't mind. He'd established who was who, and this was his exit coming up. "Canarsie," the sign said. Murch steered his car off the Belt Parkway, around the circle, and out onto Rockaway Parkway, a long, broad, flat bumpy street lined with projects, supermarkets, and row houses.

Murch lived with his mother on East 99th Street, just a little ways off Rockaway Parkway. He made his right turn, made his left turn, slowed when he came to the middle of the block, saw his mother's cab was in the driveway, and rolled on by to a parking space down near the far corner. He got his new record album—*Sounds of Indianapolis in Stereo and Hi-Fi*—out of the back seat and walked down the block to the house. It was a two-family row house, in which he and his mother lived in the three-and-a-half on the first floor and various tenants lived in the four-and-a-half on the second floor. The first floor was only a three-and-a-half because where the fourth room would have been was a garage instead.

The current tenant, a fish handler named Friedkin, was sitting in the air at the head of the outside steps to the second floor. Friedkin's wife made Friedkin sit out in the air any time there wasn't actually a blizzard or an atomic explosion going on out there. Friedkin waved, an aroma of the sea wafting from him, and called, "How you doing, boychick?"

"Yuh," said Murch. He wasn't too good at talking to people. Most of his conversations were held with cars.

He went on into the house and called, "Mom?" He stood there in the kitchen.

She'd been downstairs, in the extra room. Besides the three-and-a-half they had a semi-finished basement, what most of their neighbors considered a family room, down in the semi-dank downstairs. Murch and his mother had turned this underbelly into Murch's bedroom.

Murch's mom came upstairs now and said, "You're home."

"Look what I got," Murch said and showed her the record.

"So play it," she said.

"Okay," he said.

They went into the living room together and while Murch put the record on the turntable he said, "How come you're home so early?"

"Aahhh," she said in disgust. "Some wise-ass cop out at the airport."

"You were taking more than one passenger again," Murch said.

She flared up. "Well, why not?" she wanted to know. "This city's got a shortage of cabs, don't it? You oughta see all those people out there to the airport, they got to wait half an hour, an hour, they could fly to Europe before they could get a cab and go to Manhattan. So I try to help the situation a little. They don't care, the customers don't care, they'd have to pay the same meter anyway. And it helps me, I get two, three times the meter.

And it helps the city, it improves their goddamn public image. But try to tell a cop that. Play the record."

"How long you suspended for?"

"Two days," she said. "Play the record."

"Mom," he said, holding the tone arm above the turning record, "I wish you wouldn't take those chances. We don't have all that much dough."

"You got enough to throw it away on records," she said. "Play the record."

"If I'd known you were gonna get yourself suspended for two days—"

"You could always get yourself a job," she said. "Play the record."

Stung, Murch put the tone arm back on its rest and his hands on his hips. "Is that what you want?" he said. "You want me to get a job at the post office?"

"No, never mind me," his mother said, suddenly contrite. She went over and patted his cheek. "I know something'll come through for you pretty soon. And when you do have it, Stan, nobody on God's green earth spends it as free or as open as you do."

"Damn right," Murch said, appeased but still a little grumpy.

"Put the record on," his mother said. "Let's hear it."

"Sure."

Murch put the tone arm on the opening grooves of the record. The room filled with the shrieking of tires, the revving of engines, the grinding of gears.

They listened to side one in silence, and when it was done Murch said, "Now, that's a good record."

"I think that's one of the best, Stan," his mother said. "I really do. Let's hear the other side."

"Right."

Murch went over to the phonograph and picked up the record, and the phone rang. "Hell," he said.

"Forget it," his mother said. "Play the other side."

"Okay."

Murch put the other side on, and the ringing of the phone was buried in the sudden roar of twenty automobile engines turning over at once.

But whoever was calling wouldn't give up. In the lulls in the record the ringing cold still be heard, a disturbing presence. A racing driver going into the far turn at one hundred twenty miles an hour shouldn't have to answer the telephone.

Murch finally shook his head in disgust, shrugged at his mother, and picked up the phone. "Who is it?" he said, yelling over the sounds of the record.

A distant voice said, "Stan Murch?"

"Speaking!"

The distant voice said something else.

"What?"

The distant voice shouted, "This is Dortmunder!"

"Oh, yeah! How you doing?"

"Fine! Where do you live, in the middle of the Grand Concourse?"

"Hold on a second!" Murch shouted and put the phone down and went over to turn off the record. "I'll play it in a minute," he told his mother. "This is a guy I know, it might be a job."

"I knew something would turn up," his mother said. "Every cloud has a silver lining."

Murch went back to the phone. "Hello, Dortmunder?"

"That's a lot better," Dortmunder said. "What did you do, shut the window?"

"No, it was a record. I turned it off."

There was a long silence.

Murch said, "Dortmunder?"

"I'm here," Dortmunder said, but he sounded a little fainter than before. Then, stronger again, he said, "I wondered if you were available for a driving job."

"I sure am."

"Meet me tonight at the O. J. Bar and Grill on Amsterdam Avenue," Dortmunder said.

"Fine. What time?"

"Ten o'clock."

"I'll be there. See you, Dortmunder."

Murch hung up the phone and said to his mother, "Well, looks like we'll have some money pretty soon."

"That's good," said his mother. "Play the record."

"Right."

Murch went over and started side two from the beginning again.

7

"Toot toot," said Roger Chefwick. His three H-O gauge trains were all in motion at once on his H-O gauge track, traveling hither and yon around the basement. Relays tripped, electrical signals were given, and all sorts of things happened. Flagmen slid out of their shacks and waved their flags. Gondola cars stopped at appropriate places and filled with grain, only to stop again far away and dump their grain out again. Mailbags were picked up on the fly by mail cars. Bells rang at highway-railway crossings, bars went down, and when the train had gone by the bars went back up again. Cars coupled and uncoupled. All sorts of things went on.

"Toot toot," said Roger Chefwick.

A short and skinny man of late middle age, Chefwick was seated now on a high stool at his grand console, his practiced hands moving over the array of transformers and special switches. The waist-high plywood platform, four feet wide, flanked the wall on three sides of the basement, so that Chefwick in the middle of it all was like a man in the ultimate Cinerama. Model houses, model trees, even model mountains gave veracity to his layout. His trains traveled over bridges, through tunnels and around intricately curved multilayers of track.

"Toot toot," said Roger Chefwick.

"Roger," said his wife.

Chefwick twisted around and saw Maude standing midway down the cellar stairs. A vague, fussy, pleasant woman, Maude was his perfect mate and he knew how lucky he was to have her.

"Yes, dear," he said.

"Telephone, Roger," she said.

"Oh, dear." Chefwick sighed. "One moment," he said.

"I'll tell them," she said and turned to go back upstairs.

Chefwick faced his console again. Train number one was in the vicinity of the Chefwick freight yards, so he rerouted it from its original destination, Center City, and sent it instead through the Maude Mountain tunnel and on into the yards. Since train number two was just approaching the Rogerville station, he simply ran it onto a subsidiary track there to leave the main line open. That left train number three, currently heading through Smoke Pass. It took some intricate planning, but he finally brought it out of the Southern Mountains and shunted it onto the spur track leading to the old Seaside Mining Corporation. Then, pleased with his work, he shut off the master switches on the console and went upstairs.

The kitchen, tiny and white and warm, was full of

the aroma of fudge. Maude was at the sink, washing dishes. Chefwick said, "Mmm. Smells good."

"Be cool in just a little while," she said.

"Can't wait," he said, knowing it would please her, and went through the tiny house to the living room, where the telephone was. He sat down on the doily-covered flower-pattern sofa, picked up the phone receiver, and said mildly, "Hello?"

A rough voice said, "Chefwick?"

"Speaking."

"This is Kelp. Remember?"

"Kelp?" The name did ring a bell, but Chefwick couldn't exactly remember why. "I'm sorry, I—"

"At the bakery," the voice said.

Then he did remember. Of course, the robbery at the bakery. "Kelp!" he said, pleased to have been reminded. "How good to hear from you again. How have you been keeping yourself?"

"Little a this, little a that, you know how it is. What I—"

"Well, it certainly is good to hear your voice again. How long has it been?"

"A couple years. What I—"

"How time flies," Chefwick marveled.

"Yeah, don't it. What I—"

"But I should certainly not have forgotten your name. I must have been thinking of something else."

"Yeah, that's fine. What I—"

"But I'm keeping you from telling me why you called," Chefwick said. "I'll listen now."

Silence.

Chefwick said, "Hello?"

"Yeah," said Kelp.

"Oh, there you are."

"Yeah," said Kelp.

"Did you want something?" Chefwick asked him.

It sounded as though Kelp sighed before saying, "Yeah. I wanted something. I wanted to know are you available."

"One moment, please," Chefwick said. He put the receiver down on the end table, got to his feet, and walked out to the kitchen, where he said to his wife, "Dear, do you know offhand the state of our finances?"

Maude dried her hands on her apron, looking thoughtful, and then said, "I believe we have just about seven thousand dollars left in the checking account."

"Nothing in the basement?"

"No. I took the last three thousand at the end of April."

"Thank you," Chefwick said. He went back to the living room, sat down on the sofa, picked up the receiver, and said, "Hello?"

"Yeah," said Kelp. He sounded tired.

"I am quite interested," Chefwick said.

"Good," Kelp said, but he still sounded tired. "We're meeting tonight," he said, "at ten o'clock, at the O. J. Bar and Grill on Amsterdam Avenue."

"Fine," Chefwick said. "See you then."

"Yeah," said Kelp.

Chefwick hung up, got to his feet, went back to the kitchen, and said, "I'll be going out awhile this evening."

"Not late, I hope."

"Not tonight, I don't believe. We'll just be discussing things." Chefwick got a sly look on his face, a pixie grin on his lips. "Is that fudge ready yet?"

Maude smiled indulgently at him. "I believe you could try a piece," she said.

8

So this is your apartment!" the girl said.

"Mm, yes," said Alan Greenwood, smiling. He shut the door and pocketed the keys. "Make yourself comfortable," he said.

The girl stood in the middle of the room and turned in a big admiring circle. "Well, I must say," she said. "It certainly is well kept for a bachelor's apartment."

Greenwood, walking toward the bar, said, "I do what I can. But I do feel the lack of a woman's touch."

"It doesn't show at all," she said. "Not at all."

Greenwood switched on the fireplace. "What's yours?" he said.

"Oh," she said, shrugging, doing the coquette a little, "just anything light."

"Coming up," he said. He opened the bar portion of the bookcase and made her a Rob Roy just sweet enough to hide the deadliness of the Scotch.

When he turned, she was admiring the painting between the maroon-velvet-draped windows. "My, that's interesting," she said.

"It's the Rape of the Sabine Women," he told her. "In symbolic terms, of course. Here's your drink."

"Oh, thank you."

He raised his drink—light on the Scotch, heavy on the water—and said, "To you." Then, with hardly any pause at all, he added, "Miranda."

Miranda smiled and ducked her head in embarrassed pleasure. "To us," she whispered.

He smiled his agreement. "To us."

They drank.

"Come sit down," he said, leading her to the white sheepskin sofa.

"Oh, is that sheepskin?"

"So much warmer than leather," he said softly and took her hand, and they sat down.

Seated side by side, they gazed a moment into the fireplace, and then she said, "My, that is realistic, isn't it?"

"And no ashes," he said. "I like things—clean."

"Oh, I know what you mean," she said and smiled brightly at him.

He put his arm around her shoulders. She lifted her chin. The phone rang.

Greenwood closed his eyes, then opened them again. "Ignore it," he said.

The phone rang again.

"But it might be something important," she said.

"I have an answering service," he said. "They'll get it."

The phone rang again.

"I've thought about getting an answering service," she said. She sat forward a bit, dislodging his arm, and turned half toward him, one leg tucked under her. "Are they expensive?"

The phone rang the fourth time.

"Around twenty-five a month," he said, his smile becoming a bit forced. "But it's worth it for the convenience."

Fifth time.

"Oh, of course," she said. "And not to miss any important calls."

Sixth.

Greenwood chuckled realistically. "Of course," he said, "they aren't always as reliable as you'd like."

Seven.

"Isn't that the way with people nowadays," she said. "Nobody wants to do an honest day's work for an honest day's pay."

Eight.

"That's right."

She leaned closer to him. "Is that a tic in your eyelid? The right eye."

Nine.

He jerked a hand to his face. "Is it? I get that sometimes, when I'm tired."

"Oh, are you tired?"

Ten.

"No," he said quickly. "Not in particular. Maybe the light in the restaurant was a bit too dim, I might have been straining my—"

Eleven.

Greenwood lunged at the phone, yanked the receiver to his head, shouted, *"What is it?"*

"Hello?"

"Hello yourself! What do you want?"

"Greenwood? Alan Greenwood?"

"Who's this?" Greenwood demanded.

"Is that Alan Greenwood?"

"God damn it, yes! What do you want?" He could see from the corner of his eye that the girl had risen from the sofa, was standing looking at him.

"This is John Dortmunder."

"Dort—" He caught himself, coughed instead. "Oh," he said, much calmer. "How are things?"

"Fine. You available for a piece of work?"

Greenwood looked at the girl's face while thinking of his bank accounts. Neither prospect was pleasing. "Yes, I am," he said. He tried a smile at the girl, but it wasn't returned. She was watching him a bit warily.

"We're meeting tonight," Dortmunder said. "At ten. You free?"

"Yes, I think I am," Greenwood said. Not happily.

9

Dortmunder walked into the O. J. Bar and Grill on Amsterdam Avenue at five minutes to ten. Two of the regulars were having a game at the bowling machine, and three more were remembering Irish McCalla and Betty Page at the bar. Behind the bar stood Rollo, tall, meaty, balding, blue-jawed, in a dirty white shirt and dirty white apron.

Dortmunder had already set things up with Rollo on the phone this afternoon, but he stopped at the bar a second as a courtesy, saying, "Anybody here yet?"

"One fellow," Rollo said. "A draft beer. I don't think I know him. He's in the back."

"Thanks."

Rollo said, "You're a double bourbon, aren't you? Straight up."

Dortmunder said, "I'm surprised you remember."

"I don't forget my customers," Rollo said. "It's good to see you back again. You want, I'll bring you the bottle."

"Thanks again," Dortmunder said and walked on down past the memory trippers and past the two doors with the dog silhouettes on them and the sign on one door POINTERS and on the other door SETTERS and past the phone booth and through the green door at the back and into a small square room with a concrete floor. None of the walls could be seen because practically the whole room was taken up floor to ceiling with beer cases and liquor cases, leaving only a small opening in the middle big enough for a battered old table with a green felt top, half a dozen chairs, and one bare bulb with a round tin reflector hanging low over the table on a long black wire.

Stan Murch was sitting at the table, half a glass of draft beer in front of him. Dortmunder shut the door and said, "You're early."

"I made good time," Murch said. "Instead of goin' all the way around on the Belt, I went up Rockaway Parkway and over Eastern Parkway to Grand Army Plaza and right up Flatbush Avenue to the Manhattan Bridge. Then up Third Avenue and through the park at Seventy-ninth Street. At night you can make better time that way than if you went around the Belt Parkway and through the Battery Tunnel and up the West Side Highway."

Dortmunder looked at him. "Is that right?"

"In the daytime that way's better," Murch said. "But at night the city streets are just as good. Better."

"That's interesting," Dortmunder said and sat down.

The door opened and Rollo came in with a glass and a bottle of something that called itself Amsterdam Liquor Store Bourbon—"Our Own Brand." Rollo put the glass and the bottle down in front of Dortmunder and said, "There's a fellow outside I think is maybe with you. A sherry. Want to give him the double-o?"

Dortmunder said, "Did he ask for me?"

"Asked for a fellow name of Kelp. That the Kelp I know?"

"The same," Dortmunder said. "He'll be one of ours, send him on in."

"Will do." Rollo looked at Murch's glass. "Ready for a refill?"

"I'll string along with this for a while," Murch said.

Rollo gave Dortmunder a look and went out, and a minute later Chefwick came in, carrying a glass of sherry. "Dortmunder!" he said in surprise. "It was Kelp I talked to on the phone, wasn't it?"

"He'll be here in a minute," Dortmunder said. "You know Stan Murch?"

"I don't believe I've had the pleasure."

"Stan's our driver. Stan, this is Roger Chefwick, he's our lockman. Best in the business."

Murch and Chefwick nodded to each other, mumbling words, and Chefwick sat down at the table. "Will there be many more of us?" he said.

"Just two," Dortmunder said, and Kelp came in, carrying a glass. He looked at Dortmunder and said, "He said you had the bottle."

"Sit down," Dortmunder invited. "You all know each other, don't you?"

They did. Everybody said hello, and Kelp poured bourbon into his glass. Murch took a tiny sip of beer.

The door opened and Rollo stuck his head in.

"There's a Dewar's and water out here that asked for you," he said to Dortmunder, "but I don't know about him."

Dortmunder said, "Why not?"

"I don't think he's sober."

Dortmunder made a face. "Ask him if he calls himself Greenwood," he said, "and if he does send him on in here."

"Right." Rollo looked at Murch's beer. "You all set?" he said.

"I'm fine," Murch told him. His glass was still one-quarter full, but the beer didn't have any head any more. "Unless I could have some salt," he said.

Rollo gave Dortmunder a look. "Sure," he said and went out.

A minute later Greenwood came in, a drink in one hand and a salt shaker in the other. "The barman said the draft beer wanted this," he said. He looked high, but not drunk.

"That's me," Murch said.

Murch and Greenwood had to be introduced, and then Greenwood sat down and Murch sprinkled a little salt into his beer, which gave it back some head. He sipped at it.

Dortmunder said, "Now we're all here." He looked at Kelp. "You want to tell the story?"

"No," said Kelp. "You do it."

"All right," Dortmunder said. He told them the story, and then he said, "Any questions?"

Murch said, "We get a hundred fifty a week until we do the job?"

"Right."

"Then why do it at all?"

"Three or four weeks is all we'd get out of Major Iko," Dortmunder said. "Maybe six hundred apiece. I'd rather have the thirty thousand."

Chefwick said, "Do you want to take the emerald from the Coliseum or wait till it's on the road?"

"We'll have to decide that," Dortmunder said. "Kelp and I went over there today and it looked well guarded, but they might be even more security-conscious on the road. Why don't you go over tomorrow and see how it looks to you?"

Chefwick nodded. "Fine," he said.

Greenwood said, "Once we get this emerald, why turn it over to the good Major at all?"

"He's the only buyer," Dortmunder said. "Kelp and I have already been through all the switches we might want to pull."

"Just so we're flexible in our thinking," Greenwood said.

Dortmunder looked around. "Any more questions? No? Anybody want out? No? Good. Tomorrow you all drift over to the Coliseum and take a look at our prize, and we'll meet back here tomorrow night at the same time. I'll have the first week's living expenses from the Major by then."

Greenwood said, "Couldn't we make it earlier tomorrow night? Ten o'clock breaks into my evening pretty badly."

"We don't want it too early," Murch said. "I don't want to get caught in that rush hour traffic."

"How about eight?" Dortmunder said.

"Fine," said Greenwood.

"Fine," said Murch.

"Perfectly all right with me," said Chefwick.

"Then that's it," said Dortmunder. He pushed back his chair and got to his feet. "We'll meet back here to-morrow night."

Everybody stood. Murch finished his beer, smacked his lips, and said, "Aaaahhh!" Then he said. "Anybody want a lift anywhere?"

10

It was ten minutes to one of a weeknight, and Fifth Avenue across from the park was deserted. An occasional cab showing its off-duty sign rolled south, but that was about it. A spring drizzle was leaking out of the black sky, and the park across the way looked like the middle of a jungle.

Kelp rounded the corner and headed up the block for the embassy. He'd left the cab on Madison Avenue, but with the misty rain oozing inside his coat collar he was beginning to think he'd been overcautious. He should have had the cab drop him at the embassy door and to hell with cover. He'd concerned himself with the wrong kind of cover, a night like this.

He trotted up the embassy steps and rang the bell. He could see lights behind the first-floor windows, but it took a long while for someone to come open the door, and then it was a silent black man who motioned Kelp in with long slim fingers, shut the door after him, and led him away through several opulent rooms before finally leaving him alone in a bookcase-lined den with a pool table in its middle.

Kelp waited three minutes, standing around doing nothing, and then decided the hell with it. He got the rack from under the table, racked up the balls, selected a cue, and began to play a little rotation with himself.

He was just about to sink the eight when the door opened and Major Iko came in. "You're later than I expected," he said.

"I couldn't find a cab," Kelp said. He put down the cue, patted various pockets, and came up with a crumpled sheet of lined yellow paper. "This is the stuff we need," he said and handed the Major the sheet of paper. "You want to give me a ring when it's ready?"

"Stay a moment," the Major said. "Let me look this over."

"Take your time," Kelp said. He went back to the table and picked up the cue and sank the eight ball. Then he walked halfway around the table and dropped the nine and—on ricochet—the thirteen. The ten was already gone, so he tried for the eleven, but it glanced off the fifteen and wound up in bad position. He hunkered down, shut one eye, and began to study various lines of sight.

The Major said, "About these uniforms—"

"Just a minute," Kelp said. He sighted a little more, then stood, aimed carefully, and shot. The cue ball bounced off two cushions, grazed the eleven, and rolled into the pocket.

"Hell," Kelp said. He put the cue down and turned to Iko. "Anything wrong?"

"The uniforms," the Major said. "It says here four uniforms, but it doesn't say what kind."

"Oh, yeah, I forgot." Kelp pulled some Polaroid prints from another pocket. They showed guards at the Coliseum from various angles. "Here's some pictures," Kelp said, handing them over. "So you'll know what they look like."

The Major took the prints. "Good. And what are these numbers on the paper?"

"Everybody's suit size," Kelp said.

"Naturally. I should have realized." The Major tucked the list and prints into his pocket and smiled crookedly at Kelp. "So there really are three other men," he said.

"Sure," Kelp said. "We weren't gonna do it just the two of us."

"I realize that. Dortmunder forgot to tell me the names of the other three."

Kelp shook his head. "No, he didn't. He told me you tried to pump him on that, and he said you'd probably try with me too."

The Major, in sudden irritation, said, "Damn it, man, I ought to know who I'm hiring. This is absurd."

"No, it isn't," Kelp said. "You hired Dortmunder and me. Dortmunder and me hired the other three."

"But I need to check them out," the Major said.

"You already talked this over with Dortmunder," Kelp said. "You know what his attitude is."

"Yes, I know," said the Major.

Kelp told him anyway. "You'll start makin' up dossiers on everybody. You make up enough dossiers, you'll attract attention, maybe tip the whole thing."

The Major shook his head. "This goes against my training," he said, "against everything I know. How can you deal with a man if you don't have a dossier on him? It isn't done."

Kelp shrugged. "I don't know. Dortmunder says I should pick up this week's money."

"This is the second week," the Major said.

"That's right."

"When are you going to do the job?"

"Soon as you get us the stuff." Kelp spread his hands. "We weren't just sittin' around for a week, you know. We earned our money. Go to the Coliseum every day, sit around and work out plans every night, we've been doin' that for a week now."

"I don't begrudge the money," the Major said, though it was clear he did. "I just don't want it to drag on too long."

"Get us the stuff on that list," Kelp said, "and we'll get you your emerald."

"Good," said the Major. "Shall I see you to the door?"

Kelp glanced longingly at the pool table. "Would you mind? I'm sort of set up for the twelve, and then there's only two more balls after that."

The Major seemed both surprised and irritated, but he said, "Oh, very well. Go ahead."

Kelp smiled. "Thanks, Major." He picked up the cue, sank the twelve, sank the fourteen, took two shots to sink the fifteen, and finished off by sinking the cue ball on a three cushion rebound. "There," he said and put up the cue.

The Major let him out, and he stood ten minutes in the rain before he got a cab.

11

The New York Coliseum stands between West 58th Street and West 60th Street facing Columbus Circle on the southwest corner of Central Park in Manhattan. The Coliseum faces the park and the Maine Monument and the statue of Columbus and Huntington Hartford's Gallery of Modern Art.

On the 60th Street side, midway along the beige brick wall, there is an entrance surmounted by a large chrome number 20, and 20 West 60th Street is the address of the Coliseum staff. A blue-uniformed private guard is always on duty inside the glass doors of this entrance, day and night.

One Wednesday night in late June, at about three-twenty in the morning, Kelp came walking eastward along West 60th Street wearing a tan raincoat, and when he was opposite the Coliseum entrance he suddenly had a fit. He went rigid, and then he fell over, and then he began to thrash around on the sidewalk. He cried, "Oh! Oh!" several times, but in a husky voice that didn't carry far. There was no one else in sight, no pedestrians and no moving automobiles.

The guard had seen Kelp through the glass doors before the fit started, and knew that Kelp had not been walking as though drunk. He had in fact been walking very calmly until he had his fit. The guard hesitated a moment, frowning worriedly, but Kelp's thrashing seemed to be increasing, so at last the guard opened the door and hurried out to see what he could do to help. He squatted beside Kelp, put a hand on Kelp's twitching shoulder, and said, "Is there anything I can do, Mac?"

"Yes," Kelp said. He stopped thrashing and pointed a .38 Special Colt Cobra revolver at the guard's nose. "You can stand up very slow," Kelp said, "and you can keep your hands where I can see them."

The guard stood up and kept his hands where Kelp could see them, and out of a car across the street came Dortmunder and Greenwood and Chefwick, all dressed in uniforms exactly like the one the guard was wearing.

Kelp got to his feet, and the four marched the guard into the building. He was taken around the corner from the entrance and tied and gagged. Kelp then removed his raincoat, showing yet another uniform of the same type, and went back to take the guard's place at the door. Meanwhile Dortmunder and the other two stood around and looked at their watches. "He's late," Dortmunder said.

"He'll get there," Greenwood said.

Around at the main entrance there were two guards on duty, and at this moment they were both looking out at an automobile that had suddenly come out of nowhere and was hurtling directly toward the doors. "No!" cried one of the guards, waving his arms.

Stan Murch was behind the wheel of the car, a two-year-old Rambler Ambassador sedan, dark green, which Kelp had stolen just this morning. The car had different plates now, and other changes had also been made.

At the last possible second before the impact Murch pulled the pin on the bomb, shoved the door open, and leaped clear. He landed rolling, and continued to roll for several seconds after the sounds of the crash and the explosion.

The timing had been beautiful. No eyewitness—there were none but the two guards—would have been able to say for sure that Murch had leaped before the crash rather than been thrown clear because of it. And no one would have supposed that the sheet of flame that suddenly erupted from the car as it crashed to a stop halfway through the glass doors was not the result of the accident but had been made by the small incendiary bomb with the five-second fuse whose pin Murch had pulled just before his exit.

Nor would anyone suppose that the stains and smears on Murch's face and clothing had been carefully applied almost an hour ago in a small apartment on the Upper West Side.

The crash, at any rate, was magnificent. The car had leaped the curb, had seemed to bound twice in crossing the wide sidewalk, and had lunged into and through the glass doors on the rise, thudding to a grinding halt, half in and half out, and then bursting at once into flame. Within seconds the fire reached the gas tank—it was supposed to, having been assured by some alterations Murch had made this afternoon—and the explosion shattered what glass the car had missed.

No one in the building could have failed to hear Murch's arrival. Dortmunder and the others heard it, and they smiled at one another and moved out, leaving Kelp behind to guard the door.

Their route to the exhibit area was roundabout, involving several corridors and two flights of stairs, but when they at last opened one of the heavy metal doors leading to the second floor exhibit area, they saw their timing had been perfect. There wasn't a guard in sight.

They were all out front, by the fire. Several of them were clustered around Murch, whose head was in a guard's lap and who was obviously in shock, lying there twitching, muttering, "It wouldn't steer . . . it wouldn't steer . . ." and moving his arms vaguely, like a man trying to turn a steering wheel. Some of the other guards were standing around the blazing car, telling one another what a lucky guy that lucky guy was, and at least four of them were at four different telephones, calling hospitals and police stations and fire departments.

Inside, Dortmunder and Chefwick and Greenwood made their way quickly and silently through the exhibits toward the Akinzi display. Only a few lights were on, and in the semi-dark some of the exhibits they moved among tended toward the startling. Devil masks, warriors in spear and costume, even wildly designed tapestries, all were a lot more effective now than during normal visiting hours, with all the lights lit and lots of other people around.

When they reached the Akinzi display they went immediately to work. They'd studied this for a week now, they knew what to do and how.

There were four locks to be undone, one in the middle of each side of the glass cube, down at the base, in the steel rim between glass and floor. Once these locks were opened the glass cube could be lifted out of the way.

Chefwick had with him a small black bag of the sort country doctors used to favor, and this he now opened, revealing many slender metal tools of the sort most country doctors never saw in their lives. While Greenwood and Dortmunder stood on either side of him, watching the exit doors on the far walls and the railing of the third-floor balcony overlooking this area and the stairs and escalator toward the front of the building, where they could see the reflected red glow from the fire down in the lobby, while they kept careful watch on all this, Chefwick went to work on the locks.

The first one took three minutes, but after that he knew the system and he did all the other three in less than four minutes more. But still, seven minutes was a long time. The red glow was fading, and the noise from downstairs was ebbing; soon the guards would be coming back to their duties. Dortmunder refrained from telling Chefwick to hurry, but with difficulty. Still, he knew Chefwick was doing the best he could.

At last Chefwick whispered a shrill "Done!" Still kneeling by the last breached lock, he hurriedly put his tools back into his bag.

Dortmunder and Greenwood got on opposite sides

of the glass cube. It weighed close to two hundred pounds, and there was no way for them to get a really good grip on it. They could only press their palms against it at the edges and lift. Straining, sweating, they did so, gazing at each other's tense face through the glass, and when they got it up two feet Chefwick slid under and grabbed the emerald.

"Hurry up!" Greenwood said, his voice hoarse. "It's slipping!"

"Don't leave me in here!" Chefwick rolled quickly out from underneath.

"My palms are wet," Greenwood said, even his voice straining. "Lower it. Lower it."

"Don't let it go," Dortmunder called. "For God's sake, don't let it go."

"It won't—I can't—it's—"

The glass slid out of Greenwood's grip. With the pressure gone from the other side, Dortmunder couldn't hold it either. The glass cube dropped eighteen inches and hit the floor.

It didn't break. It went bbrrroooo*oonnnn*NNNNNNNN-NNGGGGGGGGGGGGGINGINGING*inging*ing.

Shouting from downstairs.

"Come on!" Dortmunder yelled.

Chefwick, rattled, shoved the emerald into Greenwood's hand. "Here. Take it." He grabbed up his black bag.

Guards were appearing at the head of the stairs, far away. "Hey, you!" one of them called. "You stop there, stay where you are!"

"Scatter!" Dortmunder cried and ran to the right.

Chefwick ran to the left.

Greenwood ran straight ahead.

Meanwhile, the ambulance had arrived. The police had arrived. The fire department had arrived. A uniformed policeman was trying to ask Murch questions while a white-garbed ambulance attendant was telling the policeman to leave the patient alone. Firemen were putting out the fire. Someone had taken from Murch's pocket the wallet full of false identification he had put in there half an hour ago. Murch, still apparently dazed and only semi-conscious, was repeating, "It wouldn't steer. I turned the wheel and it wouldn't steer."

"It looks to me," the policeman said, "like you panicked. Something went wrong with the steering and instead of hitting the brake you tromped on the accelerator. Happens all the time."

"Leave the patient alone," the ambulance attendant said.

Finally Murch was put on a stretcher and loaded into the ambulance and driven away, the ambulance siren screaming.

Chefwick, racing pell-mell for the nearest exit, heard the siren screaming and doubled his speed. The last thing he wanted was to spend his declining years in jail. No trains. No Maude. No fudge.

He yanked open the door, found a staircase, raced down it, found a corridor, raced along that, and suddenly found himself face to face with an entrance and a guard.

He tried to turn around while still running, dropped his bag, fell over it, and the guard came over to help him up. It was Kelp, saying, "What's wrong? Something go wrong?"

"Where's the others?"

"I don't know. Should we take off?"

Chefwick got to his feet. They both listened. There was no sound of pursuit. "We'll wait a minute or two," Chefwick decided.

"We better," Kelp said. "Dortmunder's got the keys to the car."

Dortmunder, meanwhile, had run around a thatched-roof hut and joined the chase. "Stop!" he shouted, running along in the middle of a pack of guards. Up ahead he saw Greenwood duck through a door and shut it behind himself. "Stop!" shouted Dortmunder, and the guards all around him shouted, "Stop!"

Dortmunder got to the door first. He yanked it open, held it for all the guards to run through, then shut it behind them and walked over to the nearest elevator. He rode this to the first floor, walked along a corridor, and came to the side entrance where Kelp and Chefwick were waiting. "Where's Greenwood?" he said.

"Not here," said Kelp.

Dortmunder looked around. "We better wait in the car," he said.

Meanwhile, Greenwood thought he was on the first floor but wasn't. The Coliseum, in addition to its first floor, second floor, third floor, and fourth floor, has two mezzanines, the first mezzanine and the second mezzanine. The first mezzanine is between the first and second floors, but only around the outer perimeter of the building, not in the central display area. Similarly, the second mezzanine is between the second and third floors.

Greenwood didn't know about the mezzanines. He had been on the second floor and he had taken a staircase down one flight. Some staircases in the Coliseum skip the mezzanine and go straight from the second floor to the first floor, but some other staircases include the mezzanine among their stops, and it was one of the latter kind that Greenwood had inadvertently chosen. Therefore, he now thought he was on the first floor but he was not. He was on the first mezzanine.

The first mezzanine consists of a corridor that goes all the way around the building. The staff has its offices here, there's a cafeteria, the private detective agency that furnishes the guards has its offices here, various nations maintain offices, there are storage rooms and conference rooms and miscellaneous offices. It was along this corridor that Greenwood was now running, the Balaboma Emerald clutched in his hand as he searched in vain for an exit to the street.

In his ambulance, meantime, Murch was socking his attendant on the jaw. The attendant sagged into sleep and Murch settled him on the other stretcher. Then, as the ambulance slowed to make a turn, Murch opened the rear door and stepped out onto the pavement. The ambulance tore away, siren shrieking, and Murch hailed a passing cab. "O. J. Bar and Grill," he said. "On Amsterdam."

In their other stolen car, the getaway car, Dortmunder and Kelp and Chefwick kept worriedly studying the 20

West 60th Street entrance. Dortmunder had the engine running and his foot was nervously tapping the gas pedal.

Sirens were coming this way now, police sirens.

"We can't wait much longer," Dortmunder said.

"There he is!" cried Chefwick, as the door over there opened and a man in a guard uniform came out. But then half a dozen other men in guard uniforms came out too.

"That's not him," said Dortmunder. "None of them is him." He put the getaway car in gear and got away.

Up on the first mezzanine, Greenwood was still loping along like a greyhound after the mechanical rabbit. He could hear the thundering of pursuit behind him, and now he could also hear the thundering of pursuit from around the corner in the corridor up ahead.

He stopped. He was caught and he knew it.

He looked at the emerald in his hand. Roundish, many-faceted, deeply green, a trifle smaller than a golf ball.

"Drat," said Greenwood, and he ate the emerald.

12

Rollo had loaned them a portable radio, small, transistorized, Japanese, and on it they listened to the caper on WINS, the all-news station. They heard about the daring robbery, they heard about Murch having made his escape from the ambulance, they heard the history of the Balabomo Emerald, they heard about Alan Greenwood having been arrested and charged with complicity in the robbery, and they heard that the gang had managed to get away successfully with the stone. Then they heard the weather, and then they heard a woman tell them the price of lamb chops and pork chops in the city's supermarkets, and then they turned the radio off.

Nobody said anything for a while. The air in the back room was blue with smoke, and their faces in the glare of the lightbulb looked pale and tired. Finally Murch said, "I wasn't brutal." He said it sullenly. The announcer on WINS had described the attack on the ambulance attendant as brutal. "I just popped him on the jaw," Murch said. He made a fist and swung it in a small tight arc. "Like that. That ain't brutal."

Dortmunder turned to Chefwick. "You gave Greenwood the stone."

"Definitely," said Chefwick.

"You didn't drop it on the floor someplace."

"I did not," Chefwick said. He was miffed, but they were all edgy. "I distinctly remember handing it to him."

"Why?" said Dortmunder.

Chefwick spread his hands. "I really don't know. In the excitement of the moment—I don't know why I did it. I had the bag to carry and he didn't have anything and I got rattled, so I handed it to him."

"But the cops didn't find it on him," said Dortmunder.

"Maybe he lost it," said Kelp.

"Maybe." Dortmunder looked at Chefwick again. "You wouldn't be holding out on us, would you?"

Chefwick snapped to his feet, insulted. "Search me," he said. "I insist. Search me right now. In all the years I've been in this line, in I don't know how many jobs I've been on, no one has ever impugned my honesty. Never. I insist I be searched."

"All right," Dortmunder said. "Sit down, I know you didn't take it. I'm just a little bugged, that's all."

"I insist I be searched."

"Search yourself," Dortmunder said.

The door opened and Rollo came in with a fresh glass of sherry for Chefwick and more ice for Dortmunder and Kelp, who were sharing a bottle of bourbon. "Better luck next time, boys," Rollo said.

Chefwick, the argument forgotten, sat down and sipped his sherry.

"Thanks, Rollo," Dortmunder said.

Murch said, "I could stand another beer."

Rollo looked at him. "Will wonders never cease," he said and went out again.

Murch looked around at the others. "What was that all about?"

Nobody answered him. Kelp said to Dortmunder, "What am I going to tell Iko?"

"We didn't get it," Dortmunder said.

"He won't believe me."

"That's kind of tough," Dortmunder said. "You tell him whatever you want to tell him." He finished his drink and got to his feet. "I'm going home," he said.

Kelp said, "Come with me to see Iko."

"Not on your life," Dortmunder said.

PHASE TWO

1

Dortmunder carried a loaf of white bread and a half gallon of homogenized milk over to the cashier. Because it was a Friday afternoon the supermarket was pretty full, but there weren't many people ahead of him at the speed checkout and he got through pretty quickly. The girl put the bread and milk into a large bag and he carried it out to the sidewalk with his elbows held close to his sides, which looked a little weird but not terribly so.

The date was the fifth of July, nine days since the fiasco at the Coliseum up in New York, and the place was Trenton, New Jersey. The sun was shining and the air was pleasantly hot without humidity, but Dortmunder wore a light basketball jacket over his white shirt, zipped almost all the way up. Perhaps that was why he looked so irritable and sour.

He walked a block from the supermarket, still carrying the bag with his elbows pressed to his sides, and then he stopped and put the bag on the hood of a handy parked car. He reached into the right-hand pocket of his jacket and pulled out a can of tuna fish and dropped it into the bag. He reached into the left-hand pocket and pulled out two packets of beef bouillon cubes and dropped them into the bag. He reached into his left-side trouser pocket and pulled out a tube of toothpaste and dropped that into the bag. Then he zipped open his jacket and reached into his left armpit and took out a package of sliced American cheese and dropped that into the bag. And finally he reached into his right armpit and took out a package of sliced baloney and dropped that into the bag. The bag was now much more full than before, and he picked it up and carried it the rest of the way home.

Home was a fleabag residence hotel downtown. He paid an extra two dollars a week for a room with a sink and a hotplate, but he made up for it a dozen times over in the money saved by eating at home.

Home. Dortmunder walked into his room and gave it a dirty look and put his groceries away.

The place was neat, anyway. Dortmunder had learned about neatness during his first stretch and had never gotten out of the habit. It was easier to live in a neat place, and having things orderly and clean made even a gray crapper stall like this bearable.

For a time, for a time.

Dortmunder put water on for instant coffee and then sat down to read the paper he'd glommed from the head this morning. Nothing in it, nothing interesting. Greenwood hadn't made the papers for almost a week now, and nothing else in the world caught Dortmunder's attention.

He was looking for a score. The three hundred bucks he'd received from Major Iko was long since gone and he'd really been scrimping ever since. He'd reported in to the parole office here as soon as he'd hit town—no point making unnecessary trouble for himself—and they'd gotten him some sort of cockamamie job at a municipal golf course. He worked there one afternoon, trimming the edges of a green, the color reminding him of the stinking Balabomo Emerald, and wound up with a sweet sunburn on the back of his neck. That was enough of that. Since then he'd been making do on slim pickings.

Like last night. Out walking around, looking for whatever might come his way, he'd hit on one of those twenty-four-hour laundromat places, and the attendant, a chubby old woman in a gray faded flower-print dress, was sitting in a blue plastic chair sound asleep. In he'd gone and quietly tapped the machines one by one and walked out with twenty-three dollars and seventy-five cents in quarters in his pockets, damn near weight enough to pull his pants off. If he'd had to run away from a cop right then it would have been no contest.

He was sipping his instant coffee and reading the funnies when the knock came at the door. He started, looking instinctively at the window, trying to remember if there was a fire escape out there or not, and then he remembered he wasn't wanted for anything right now and he shook his head in irritation at himself and got up and walked over and opened the door, and it was Kelp.

"You're a tough man to find," Kelp said.

"Not tough enough," Dortmunder said. He jerked a thumb over his shoulder and said, "Come in." Kelp walked in and Dortmunder shut the door after him and said, "What now? Another hot caper?"

"Not exactly," Kelp said. He looked around the room. "Livin' high," he commented.

"I always throw it around like this," Dortmunder said. "Nothing but the best for me. What do you mean, not exactly?"

"Not exactly *another* caper," Kelp explained.

"What do you mean, not exactly *another* caper?"

"The same one," Kelp said.

Dortmunder looked at him. "The emerald again?"

"Greenwood stashed it," Kelp said.

"The hell," Dortmunder said.

"I'm only telling you what Iko told me," Kelp said. "Greenwood told his lawyer he stashed the stone, and sent the lawyer to tell Iko. Iko told me and I'm telling you."

"Why?" Dortmunder asked him.

"We still got a chance for our thirty gee," Kelp said. "And the hundred fifty a week again while we get set up."

"Set up for what?"

"To spring Greenwood," Kelp said.

Dortmunder made a face. "Somebody around here is hearing bells," he said. He went over and picked up his coffee and drank.

Kelp said, "Greenwood's for it and he knows it. His lawyer says the same thing, he doesn't stand a chance to beat the rap. And they'll give him the book because they're sore about the stone being gone. So either he turns the stone over to them to lighten the sentence or he turns it over to us for springing him. So all we have to do is bust him out and the stone is ours. Thirty gee, just like that."

Dortmunder frowned. "Where is he?"

"In jail," Kelp said.

"I know that," Dortmunder said. "I mean, which jail? The Tombs?"

"Naw. There was trouble, so they moved him out of Manhattan."

"Trouble? What kind of trouble?"

"Well, we were white men stealing the black man's emerald, so a lot of excitable types from Harlem took the subway downtown and made a fuss. They wanted to lynch him."

"Lynch Greenwood?"

Kelp shrugged. "I don't know where they learn stuff like that," he said.

"We were stealing it for Iko," Dortmunder said. "*He's* black."

"Yeah, but nobody knows that."

"All you have to do is look at him," Dortmunder said.

Kelp shook his head. "I mean, nobody knows about him being behind the heist."

"Oh." Dortmunder walked around the room, gnawing the knuckle of his right thumb. It was what he did when thinking. He said, "Where is he, then? What jail is he in?"

"You mean Greenwood?"

Dortmunder stopped pacing and looked at him. "No," he said heavily. "I mean King Farouk."

Kelp looked bewildered. "King Farouk? I haven't heard of him in years. Is he in the can somewhere?"

Dortmunder sighed. "I meant Greenwood," he said.

"What's this about—"

"It was sarcasm," Dortmunder said. "I won't do it again. What jail is Greenwood in?"

"Oh, some dinky can out on Long Island."

Dortmunder studied him suspiciously. Kelp had said that too offhand, he'd thrown it away a little too casually. "Some dinky can?" he said.

"It's a county jug or something," Kelp said. "They're holding him there till the trial."

"Too bad he couldn't get bail," Dortmunder said.

"Maybe the judge could read his mind," Kelp said.

"Or his record," Dortmunder said. He walked around the room some more, gnawing his thumb, thinking.

Kelp said, "We get a second shot at it, that's all. What's to worry about?"

"I don't know," Dortmunder said. "But when a job turns bad I like to leave it alone. Why throw good time after bad?"

"Do you have anything else on the fire?" Kelp asked him.

"No."

Kelp gestured, calling attention to the room. "And

from the looks of things," he said, "you ain't flush. At the very worst, we go back on Iko's payroll again."

"I guess so," Dortmunder said. The doubts still nagged him, but he shrugged and said, "What have I got to lose? You got a car with you?"

"Naturally."

"Can you operate this one?"

Kelp was insulted. "I could operate that Caddy," he said indignantly. "The damn thing wanted to operate itself, that was the trouble."

"Sure," said Dortmunder. "Help me pack."

2

Major Iko sat at his desk, shuffling dossiers. There was the dossier on Andrew Philip Kelp, the first one he'd had drawn up at the very beginning of this affair, and there was the dossier on John Archibald Dortmunder, drawn up when Kelp first suggested Dortmunder to head the operation. There was also the dossier on Alan George Greenwood, which the Major had requested the instant he'd learned the man's name in the course of television reports of the robbery. And now there was the fourth dossier to be added to what was becoming a bulging file, the Balabomo File, the dossier on Eugene Andrew Prosker, attorney at law.

Greenwood's attorney, in fact. The dossier described a fifty-three-year-old lawyer with his own one-man office in a sagging building way downtown near the courts and with a large home on several wooded areas in an extremely expensive and restricted area of Connecticut. E. Andrew Prosker, as he called himself, had all the appurtenances of a rich man, including in a Long Island stable two racing horses of which he was part owner and in an East 63rd Street apartment a blond mistress of whom he thought himself sole owner. He had a reputation for shadiness in the Criminal Courts Building, and his clients tended to be among the more disreputable of society's anti-bodies, but no public complaint had ever been lodged against him and within certain specific boundaries he did appear to be trustworthy. As one former client reportedly had said of Prosker, "I'd trust Andy alone with my sister all night long, if she didn't have more than fifteen cents on her."

The three photos in the dossier showed a paunchy, jowly sort of a man with a loose cheery smile that implied laxness of mind and body. The eyes were too shadowed for their expression to be seen clearly in any of the pictures. It was hard to gibe that happy-go-lucky school's-out smile with the facts in the dossier.

The dossiers pleased the Major. He liked to touch them, to shuffle them around, reread documents in them, study photos. It gave him a feeling of solidity, of doing the familiar and the known. The dossiers were like a security blanket, in that they were not functional in the normal sense. They didn't keep the Major physically warm, they just soothed his fear of the unknown by their presence.

The secretary, light reflecting from his glasses, opened the door and said, "Two gentlemen to see you, sir. Mr. Dortmunder and Mr. Kelp."

The Major tucked the dossiers away in a drawer. "Show them in," he said.

Kelp seemed unchanged when he came somewhat

jauntily in, but Dortmunder seemed thinner and more tired than before, and he'd been both thin and tired to begin with. Kelp said, "Well, I brought him."

"So I see." The Major got to his feet. "Good to see you again, Mr. Dortmunder," he said. He wondered if he should offer to shake hands.

"I hope it's good," Dortmunder said. He gave no indication he expected a handshake. He dropped into a chair, put his hands on his knees, and said, "Kelp tells me we get another chance."

"More than we anticipated," the Major said. Kelp had also taken a seat now, so the Major sat down again behind the desk. He put his elbows on the desk and said, "Frankly, I had suspected you of perhaps taking the emerald yourself."

"I don't want an emerald," Dortmunder said. "But I'll take some bourbon."

The Major was surprised. "Of course," he said. "Kelp?"

"I don't like to see a man drink alone," Kelp said. "We both like it with a little ice."

The Major reached out to ring for his secretary, but the door opened first and the secretary came in, saying, "Sir, a Mr. Prosker is here."

"See what he'll have to drink," said the Major.

The secretary reflected blank light. "Sir?"

"Bourbon and ice for these two gentlemen," said the Major, "and a strong Scotch and water for me."

"Yes, sir," said the secretary.

"And send Mr. Prosker in."

"Yes, sir."

The secretary withdrew and the Major heard a voice boom, "Jack Daniels!" He was about to reach for his dossiers when he remembered that Jack Daniels was a kind of American whiskey.

An instant later Prosker came striding in, smiling, carrying a black attaché case, saying, "Gentlemen, I'm late. I hope this won't take long. You're Major Iko, I take it."

"Mr. Prosker." The Major got to his feet and took the lawyer's outstretched hand. He recognized Prosker from the dossier photos, but now he saw what the photos hadn't been able to show, the thing that bridged the gulf between Prosker's easygoing appearance and rough-riding record. It was Prosker's eyes. The mouth laughed and said words and lulled everybody, but the eyes just hung back and watched and made no comment at all.

The Major made the introductions, and Prosker handed both Dortmunder and Kelp his business card, saying, "In case you're ever in need, though of course we hope it won't come to that." And chuckled, and winked. Then they all sat down again and were about to get to it when the secretary came back in with their drinks on a tray. But that too was finally taken care of, the secretary retired, the door was shut, and Prosker said, "Gentlemen, I rarely give my clients advice that doesn't come out of the lawbooks, but with our friend Greenwood I made an exception. 'Alan,' I said, 'my advice to you is tie some bedsheets together and get the hell out of here.' Gentlemen, Alan Greenwood was caught green-handed, as you might say. They didn't find this emerald of yours on him, but they didn't need to. He was trotting around the Coliseum in a guard uniform and he was identified by half a dozen guards as being one of the men spotted in the vicinity of the Balabomo Emerald at the time of the robbery. They have Greenwood cold, there isn't a thing I can do for him, and I told him so. His only hope is to depart the premises."

Dortmunder said, "What about the emerald?"

Prosker spread his hands. "He says he got away with it. He says your associate Chefwick handed it to him, he says he hid it on his person before being captured, and he says it is now hidden away in a safe place that no one knows about but him."

Dortmunder said, "And the deal is, we break him out and he hands over the emerald for everybody to split again, same as before."

"Absolutely."

"And you'll be liaison."

Prosker smiled. "Within limits," he said. "I do have to protect myself."

Dortmunder said, "Why?"

"Why? Because I don't want to be arrested, I don't want to be disbarred, I don't want to be occupying the cell next to Greenwood."

Dortmunder shook his head. "No, I mean why be liaison at all. Why stick your neck out even a little bit?"

"Oh, well." Prosker's smile turned modest. "One does what one can for one's clients. And, of course, if you do rescue young Greenwood he'll be able to afford a much stiffer legal fee, won't he?"

"Sort of an illegal fee, this time," Kelp said and cackled.

Dortmunder turned to the Major. "And we go back on the payroll, is that right?"

The Major nodded reluctantly. "It's becoming more expensive than I anticipated," he said, "but I suppose I have to go on with it."

"Don't strain yourself, Major," Dortmunder said.

The Major said, "Perhaps you don't realize, Dortmunder, but Talabwo is not a rich country. Our gross national product has only recently topped twelve million dollars. We cannot afford to support foreign criminals the way some countries can."

Dortmunder bristled. "What countries, Major?"

"I name no names."

"What are you hinting at, Major?"

"Now, now," Prosker said, being jolly, "let's not have displays of nationalism. I'm sure we're all of us patriots in our various ways, but the important thing at the moment is Alan Greenwood and the Balabomo Emerald. I have some things . . ." He picked up his attaché case, put it in his lap, opened the snaps, and lifted the lid. "Shall I give these to you, Dortmunder?"

"What have you got?"

"Some maps that Greenwood made up of the interior of the prison. Some photos of the outside that I took myself. A sheet of suggestions from Greenwood, concerning guard movements and so on." Prosker took three bulky manila envelopes from his attaché case and handed them over to Dortmunder.

There was a little more talk after that, mostly killing time while they killed their drinks, and then everybody stood up and shook hands and they all left, and Major

Iko stayed in his office and chewed the inside of his cheek, which is what he frequently did when he was angry at himself or worried.

At the moment he was angry at himself *and* worried. That had been a slip, to tell Dortmunder how poor Talabwo was. Dortmunder had been distracted by chauvinism at the time, but would he remember it later and begin to wonder? Begin to put two and two together?

The Major went over to the window and looked down at Fifth Avenue and the park. Usually that view gave him pleasure, knowing just how expensive it was and how many millions of human beings the world over could not possibly afford it, but at the moment he was too troubled to enjoy selfish pleasures. He saw Dortmunder and Kelp and Prosker emerge from the building, saw them stand talking briefly on the sidewalk, saw Prosker laugh, saw them all shake hands, saw Prosker flag a cab and be driven away, saw Dortmunder and Kelp cross the street and enter the park. They walked slowly away along a blacktop path, coveys of children ebbing around them as they talked together, Dortmunder carrying the three bulky manila envelopes in his left hand. Major Iko watched them till they were out of sight.

3

N ice place," Kelp said.

"It's not bad," Dortmunder admitted. He shut the door and pocketed the key.

It wasn't bad. It was a lot better than the place in Trenton. This one, a furnished one-and-a-half on West 74th Street half a block from the park, was a long step up from the place in Trenton.

To begin with, there wasn't any bed. The room in Trenton had been half the size of this room, and the available space had been dominated by a heavy old brass bed with a faded blue cotton spread on it. Here there was no visible bed at all, only a tasteful sofa that opened up at night into a comfortable double bed.

But the improvements over Trenton didn't stop there. Where in Trenton Dortmunder had had a hotplate, here he had an honest-to-God kitchenette, with a stove and a refrigerator and cabinets and dishes and a drain rack. Where in Trenton his one window had looked out on a narrow airshaft, here his two windows looked out on the rear of the building, so he could lean out if he wanted and see a couple of small trees way down to the right, some bushes and grass in various back yards, a barbecue pit off to the left, some deck chairs with occasional occupants, all sorts of interesting things. And a fire escape, in case there was ever a reason why he didn't want to leave through the front door.

But the main thing that this apartment had over the place in Trenton was air conditioning. The unit was built right into the wall under the left-hand window, and Dortmunder kept it going night and day. Outside, New York City was suffering July, but in here it was perpetual May. And a lovely May, at that.

Kelp commented on it right away, saying, "Nice and cool in here." He wiped sweat from his forehead onto the back of his hand.

"That's what I like about it," Dortmunder said. "Drink?"

"You bet."

Kelp followed him to the kitchenette and stood in the doorway while Dortmunder got out ice cubes, glasses, bourbon. Kelp said, "What do you think of Prosker?"

Dortmunder opened a drawer, reached into it, held up a corkscrew, looked at Kelp, put the corkscrew away again.

Kelp nodded. "Me too. That's a geometric figure, that bird, he don't exist without an angle."

"Just so it's Greenwood he puts it to," Dortmunder said.

"You think that's what it is? We get the rock, get

paid, he turns Greenwood back in and takes the thirty grand for himself."

"I don't know what he's up to," Dortmunder said. "Just so he isn't up to it with me." He handed Kelp his drink and they went back to the living room and sat on the sofa.

Kelp said, "We'll need them both, I suppose."

Dortmunder nodded. "One to drive, one to open locks."

"You want to call them, or you want me to?"

"This time," Dortmunder said, "I'll call Chefwick and you call Murch."

"Fine. Shall I go first?"

"Go ahead."

The phone had come with the apartment and was on the stand next to Kelp. He looked up Murch's number in his little book, dialed, and Dortmunder faintly heard two rings and then clearly heard what sounded like the Long Island Expressway.

Kelp said, "Murch?" He looked at Dortmunder, baffled, and then louder he said, "Murch?" He shook his head at Dortmunder and shouted into the phone, "It's me! Kelp! *Kelp!*" He kept shaking his head. "Yeah," he said. "*I said yeah! Go ahead!*" Then he cupped the mouthpiece and said to Dortmunder, "Is it a phone in his car?"

"It's a record," Dortmunder said.

"It's a what?"

Dortmunder heard the sudden silence from the phone. "He turned it off," he said.

Kelp took the phone away from his head and studied it as though the thing had just bit him on the ear. A tinny voice came from it, saying, "Kelp? Hello?"

Kelp, a bit reluctantly, put the phone against his head again. "Yeah," he said doubtfully. "That you, Stan?"

Dortmunder got to his feet and went out to the kitchenette and began to put cheese spread on Ritz Crackers. He did about a dozen of them, put them on a plate, and brought them back in to the living room, where Kelp was just finishing up the conversation. Dortmunder put the plate of crackers on the coffee table, Kelp hung up the phone, Dortmunder sat down, and Kelp said, "He'll meet us at the O. J. at ten."

"Good."

"What kind of a record?"

"Car noises," Dortmunder said. "Have some cheese and crackers."

"How come car noises?"

"How do I know? Hand me the phone, I'll call Chefwick."

Kelp handed him the phone. "At least Chefwick doesn't make car noises," he said.

Dortmunder dialed Chefwick's number, and his wife answered. Dortmunder said, "Is Roger there? This is Dortmunder."

"One moment, please."

Dortmunder spent the time eating cheese and crackers, washing them down with bourbon on the rocks. After a while, faintly, he could hear a voice saying, "Toot toot." He looked at Kelp, but he didn't say anything.

The toot-toot voice came closer, then stopped. There

was the sound of the phone being picked up, and then Chefwick's voice said, "Hello?"

Dortmunder said, "You know that idea we had that didn't work out?"

"Oh, yes," Chefwick said. "I remember it well."

"Well, there's a chance we can make it work after all," Dortmunder said. "If you're still interested."

"Well, I'm intrigued, naturally," Chefwick said. "I suppose it's too complicated to go into over the phone."

"It sure is," Dortmunder said. "Ten o'clock at the O. J.?"

"That will be fine," Chefwick said.

"See you."

Dortmunder hung up and handed the phone back to Kelp, who put it back on its stand and said, "See? No car noises."

"Have some cheese and crackers," Dortmunder said.

4

Dortmunder and Kelp walked into the O. J. Bar and Grill at one minute after ten. The same regular customers were draped in their usual positions on the bar, watching the television set, looking not quite as real as the figures in a wax museum. Rollo was wiping glasses with a towel that once was white.

Dortmunder said, "Hi," and Rollo nodded. Dortmunder said, "Anybody else here yet?"

"The beer and salt is back there," Rollo said. "You expecting the sherry?"

"Yeah."

"I'll send him along when he comes in. You boys want a bottle and glasses and some ice, right?"

"Right."

"I'll bring it on in."

"Thanks."

They walked on into the back room and found Murch there reading his Mustang owner's manual. Dortmunder said, "You're early again."

"I tried a different route," Murch said. He put the owner's manual down on the green felt tabletop. "I went over to Pennsylvania Avenue and up Bushwick and Grand and over the Williamsburg Bridge and straight up Third Avenue. It seemed to work out pretty well." He picked up his beer and drank three drops.

"That's good," Dortmunder said. He and Kelp sat down, and Rollo came in with the bourbon and glasses. While he was putting them down, Chefwick came in. Rollo said to him, "You're a sherry, right?"

"Yes, thank you."

"Done."

Rollo went out, not bothering to ask Murch if he was ready for another, and Chefwick sat down, saying, "I'm certainly intrigued. I don't see how the emerald job can come back to life again. It's lost, isn't it?"

"No," Dortmunder said. "Greenwood hid it."

"In the Coliseum?"

"We don't know where. But he clouted it somewhere, and that means we can get back on the track."

Murch said, "There's a gimmick in this somewhere, I can smell it."

"Not a gimmick exactly," Dortmunder said. "Just another heist. Two for the price of one."

"What do we heist?"

"Greenwood."

Murch said, "Hah?"

"Greenwood," Dortmunder repeated, and Rollo came in with Chefwick's sherry. He went out again and Dortmunder said, "Greenwood's price is we bust him out.

His lawyer tells him there's no way to beat the rap, so he's got to beat a retreat instead."

Chefwick said, "Does that mean we're going to break *into* jail?"

"In and back out," Kelp said.

"We hope," Dortmunder said.

Chefwick smiled in a dazed sort of way and sipped at his sherry. "I never thought I'd be breaking *into* jail," he said. "It raises interesting questions."

Murch said, "You want me to drive, huh?"

"Right," said Dortmunder.

Murch frowned and drank a whole mouthful of beer.

Dortmunder said, "What's wrong?"

"Me sitting in a car, late at night, outside a jail, gunning the engine. I don't feature it. It don't raise any interesting questions for *me* at all."

"If we can't work it out," Dortmunder said, "we won't do it."

Kelp said to Murch, "None of us wants to go into that jail for more than a minute or two. If it looks like years, don't worry, we'll throw it over."

Murch said, "I got to be careful, that's all. I'm the sole support of my mother."

Dortmunder said, "Doesn't she drive a cab?"

"There's no living in that," Murch said. "She just does that to get out of the house, meet people."

Chefwick said, "What sort of jail is this?"

"We'll all go out there, one time or another, take a look at it," Dortmunder told him. "In the meantime, this is what I've got." He began to spread out on the table the contents of the three manila envelopes.

5

Kelp was shown to a different room this time, but he said, "Hey! Hold on just a minute."

The ebony man with the long thin fingers turned back in the doorway, his face expressionless. "Sir?"

"Where's the pool table?"

Still no expression. "Sir?"

Kelp made motions like a man operating a cue. "The pool table," he said. "Pocket billiards. The green table with the holes in it."

"Yes, sir. That's in a different room."

"Right," said Kelp. "That's the room I want. Lead me to it."

The ebony man didn't seem to know how to take that. He still had no expression on his face, but he just stood there in the doorway, not doing anything.

Kelp walked over to him and made shooing motions. "Let's go," he said. "I feel like dropping a few."

"I'm not sure—"

"I'm sure," Kelp told him. "Don't you worry about it, I'm positive. Just you lead me there."

"Yes, sir," said the ebony man doubtfully. He led the way to the room with the pool table in it, shut the door after Kelp, and went away.

The one ball being blind after the break, Kelp decided to play straight pool this time. He dropped twelve balls with only four misses and was taking aim at the one at last when the Major came in.

Kelp put the cue down on the table. "Hi, Major. Got another list for you."

"It's about time," said the Major. He frowned at the pool table, and he seemed irritated by something.

Kelp said, "What do you mean, about time? Less than three weeks."

"It took less than two weeks last time," the Major said.

Kelp said, "Major, they don't guard coliseums the way they guard jails."

"All I know is," said the Major, "I have so far paid out three thousand three hundred dollars in salaries, not counting the cost of materials and supplies, and so far I have nothing to show for it."

"That much?" Kelp shook his head. "It sure mounts up, doesn't it? Well, here's the list."

"Thank you."

The Major sourly studied the list while Kelp went back to the table and sank the one ball, leaving the nine and the thirteen. He missed a try for the nine but wound up with perfect position on the thirteen. He dropped the thirteen with enough back spin on the cue ball to practically put it inside his shirt, and the Major said, "A truck?"

"We're going to need one," Kelp said. He sighted on the nine. "And it can't be hot, or I'd go out and get one myself."

"But a truck," said the Major. "That's an expensive item."

"Yes, sir. But if things work out, you'll be able to sell it back when we're done with it."

"This will take a while," the Major said. He scanned the list. "The other things should be no problem. You're going to scale a wall, eh?"

"That's what they've got there," Kelp said. He hit the cue ball, which hit the nine, and everything dropped. Kelp shook his head and put up the cue.

The Major was still frowning at the list. "This truck doesn't have to be fast?"

"We don't want to outrun anybody in it, no."

"So it doesn't have to be new. A used truck."

"With a clean registration we can show," Kelp said.

"What if I rent one?"

"If you can rent a truck that it won't get back to you if things go wrong, you go right ahead. Just remember what we're using it for."

"I'll remember," the Major said. He glanced at the pool table. "If you're finished with your game . . ."

"Unless you'd like to try it with me."

"I'm sorry," the Major said with a dead smile, "I don't play."

6

From his cell window Alan Greenwood could see the blacktopped exercise yard and the whitewashed outer wall of Utopia Park Prison. Beyond that wall hunkered the small Long Island community of Utopia Park, a squat flat Monopoly board of housing, shopping centers, schools, churches, Italian restaurants, Chinese restaurants, and orthopedic shoe stores, bisected by the inevitable rails of the Long Island Railroad. Inside the wall sat and stood and scratched those adjudged to be dangerous to that Monopoly board, including the gray-garbed group of shuffling men out there in the exercise yard at the moment and Alan Greenwood, who was watching them and thinking how much they looked like people waiting for a subway. Next to the cell window someone had scratched into the cement wall the question "What did the White Rabbit know?" Greenwood was yet to figure that one out.

Utopia Park Prison was a county jug, but most of its inmates belonged to the state, the county possessing three newer jugs of its own and no longer needing this one. The overflow of various state prisons was here, plus various charged men from upstate who'd won change of venue for their trials, plus some overflow from the boroughs of New York City, plus some special cases like Greenwood. No one was here for long, no one ever would be here long, so the joint lacked the usual complex society prisoners normally set up within the walls to keep themselves in practice for civilization. No pecking order, in other words.

Greenwood was spending most of his time at the window because he liked neither his cell nor his cellmate. Both were gray, scabrous, dirty, and old. The cell merely existed, but the cellmate consumed a lot of the hours in picking at things between his toes and then smelling his fingertips. Greenwood preferred to watch the exercise yard and the wall and the sky. He had been here nearly a month now, and his patience was wearing thin.

The door clanged. Greenwood turned around, saw his cellmate on the top bunk smelling his fingertips, and saw a guard standing in the doorway. The guard looked like the cellmate's older brother, but at least he had his shoes on. He said "Greenwood. Visitor."

"Goody."

Greenwood went out, the door clanged again, Greenwood and the guard walked down the metal corridor and down the metal spiral stairs and along the other metal corridor and through two doors, both of which had to be unlocked by people on the outside and both of which were locked again in his wake. This was followed by a plastic corridor painted green and then a room painted light brown in which Eugene Andrew Prosker sat and smiled on the other side of a wall of wire mesh.

Greenwood sat opposite him. "How goes the world?"

"It turns," Prosker assured him. "It turns."

"And how's my appeal coming?" Greenwood didn't mean an appeal to any court, but his request for deliverance to his former pards.

"Coming well," Prosker said. "I wouldn't be surprised if you heard something by morning."

Greenwood smiled. "That's good news," he said. "And believe me I'm ready for good news."

"All your friends ask of you," Prosker said, "is that you meet them halfway. I know you'll want to do that, won't you?"

"I sure will," Greenwood said, "and I mean to try."

"You should try more than once," Prosker told him. "Anything that's worth trying is worth trying three times at the very least."

"I'll remember that," Greenwood said. "You haven't given my friends any of the other details, I guess."

"No," Prosker said. "As we decided, it would probably be best to wait till you're free before going into all that."

"I suppose so," Greenwood said. "Did you get my stuff out of the apartment?"

"All seen to," Prosker said. "All safely in storage under your friend's name."

"Good." Greenwood shook his head. "I hate to give up that apartment," he said. "I had it just the way I wanted."

"You'll be changing a lot of things once we get you out of here," Prosker reminded him.

"That's right. Sort of starting a new life almost. Turning over a new leaf. Becoming a new man."

"Yes," said Prosker, unenthusiastically. He didn't like taking unnecessary chances with double entendres. "Well, it's certainly encouraging to see you talking like this," he said, getting to his feet, gathering up his attaché case. "I hope we'll have you out of here in no time."

"So do I," Greenwood said.

7

At two twenty-five A.M., the morning after Prosker's visit to Greenwood, the stretch of Northern State Parkway in the vicinity of the Utopia Park exit was very nearly empty. Only one vehicle was in the area, a large dirty truck with a blue cab and a gray body, the words "Parker's Rent-a-Truck" in a white-lettered oval on both cab doors. Major Iko had done the renting, through untraceable middlemen, just this afternoon, and Kelp was doing the driving at the moment, heading east out of New York. As he slowed now for the exit, Dortmunder, in the seat beside him, leaned forward to look at his watch in the dashboard light and say, "We're five minutes early."

"I'll take it slow on the bumpy streets," Kelp said, "on account of everything in back."

"We don't want to be there too early," Dortmunder said.

Kelp steered the cumbersome truck off the parkway

and around the curve of the exit ramp. "I know," he said. "I know."

In the prison at this same time Greenwood was also looking at his watch, the green hands in the darkness telling him he still had half an hour to wait. Prosker had told him Dortmunder and the others wouldn't be making their move until three o'clock. He shouldn't do anything too early that might tip their mitts.

Twenty-five minutes later the rental truck, lights off, rolled to a stop in the parking lot of an A&P three blocks from the prison. Street lights at corners were the only illumination anywhere in this part of Utopia Park, and the cloudy sky made the night even blacker. You could just barely see your hand in front of your face.

Kelp and Dortmunder got out of the cab and moved cautiously around to open the doors at the rear of the truck. The interior of the truck was pitch black. While Dortmunder helped Chefwick to jump down onto the asphalt, Murch handed a ten-foot ladder out to Kelp. Kelp and Dortmunder stood the ladder up against the side of the truck while Murch handed out to Chefwick a coil of gray rope and his little black bag. They were all dressed in dark clothing and they communicated in whispers.

Dortmunder took the coil of rope and went first up the ladder, Chefwick following him. Kelp, at the bottom, held the ladder steady until they were both on top of the truck and then pushed the ladder up after them. Dortmunder laid the ladder lengthwise on the truck top and then he and Chefwick lay down on either side of it, like Boccaccio characters flanking a sword. Kelp, once the ladder was up, went around back again and shut the doors, then got back into the cab, started the engine, and drove the truck slowly around the A&P and out to the street. He didn't turn the headlights on.

In the prison Greenwood, looking at his watch and seeing it was five minutes to three, decided the time had come. He sat up, throwing the covers off, showing he was already fully dressed except for shoes. He put his shoes on now, got to his feet, looked at the sleeping man in the top bunk for a few seconds—the old man was snoring slightly, mouth open—and then Greenwood hit him in the nose.

The old man's eyes popped open, round and white, and for two or three seconds he and Greenwood stared at each other, their faces no more than a foot apart. Then the old man blinked, and his hand sidled up from under the blanket to touch his nose, and he said, in surprise and pain, "Ow."

Greenwood, shouting at the top of his voice, bellowed, *"Stop picking your feet!"*

The old man sat up, his eyes getting rounder and rounder. His nose was starting to bleed. He said, "What? What?"

Still at top volume, Greenwood roared, *"And stop sniffing your fingers!"*

The old man's fingers were still against his nose, but now he took them away and looked at them, and there was blood on the tips. "Help," he said, in a very quiet voice, tentatively, as though to be sure that was the word he was looking for. Then, apparently sure, he let fly with a raucous string of helps, putting his head back, squeezing his eyes shut, yipping like a terrier, *"Helphelphelp-helphelphelphelphelp—"* etc.

"I can't take it any more," Greenwood raged, taking the baritone part. *"I'll break your neck for you!"*

"Helphelphelphelphelphelphelp—"

Lights went on. Guards were shouting. Greenwood began to swear, to tramp back and forth, to wave his fists in the air. He yanked the blanket off the old man, wadded it up, threw it back at him. He grabbed the old man's ankle and began to squeeze it as though he thought it was the old man's neck.

The big clang came that meant the long iron bar across all the cell doors on this side of the tier had been lifted. Greenwood yanked the old man out of bed by his ankle, being careful not to hurt him, clutched him around the neck with one hand, raised his other fist high, and stood posed like that, bellowing, until the cell door opened and three guards came rushing in.

Greenwood didn't make it easy for them. He didn't punch any of them because he didn't want them to punch him back with truncheons and make him unconscious, but he did keep poking the old man at them, making it difficult for them to come around through the narrow cell and get their hands on him.

Then, all at once, he subsided. He released the old man, who promptly sat down on the floor and began to clutch his own neck, and he stood there slump-shouldered, vague-eyed. "I don't know," he said fuzzily, shaking his head. "I don't know."

The guards put their hands on his arms. "We know,"

one of them said, and the second said quietly to the third, "Flipped out. I wouldn't of thought it from him."

Not too many walls away, the rented truck had rolled silently and blackly to a stop against the outer wall of the prison. There were towers at both corners of the wall and there was a great deal of light in other parts of the wall, such as the part around the main entrance and the part near the exercise yard, but here there was silence and darkness only intermittently broken by a searchlight sweeping along the length of the wall from the inside. The reason was, there were no cells nor entrances near this part of the wall at all. On the other side of this wall, according to Greenwood's maps, were buildings housing the prison heating plant, the laundry, the kitchens and dining halls, the chapels, various storage sheds and the like. No part of the wall was left totally unguarded, but the guard in this area was the most perfunctory. Besides, with such a transient prison population as that at Utopia Park Prison, escapes were very rarely attempted.

As soon as the truck came to a stop, Dortmunder got to his feet and leaned the ladder against the wall. It reached almost to the top. He hurried up it while Chefwick held it steady, and at the top he peeked over, watching for the searchlight. It came, it showed him a layout of building roofs that matched Greenwood's map, and he ducked out of sight just before it swept past the spot where his head had been. He went back down the ladder and whispered, "It's all right."

"Good," Chefwick whispered.

Dortmunder joggled the ladder to be sure it would hold still with no one at the bottom to mind it, and then

he went back up, Chefwick this time following close behind him. Dortmunder carried the coil of rope over one
shoulder, Chefwick toted his black bag. Chefwick moved
with an agility surprising in a man of his appearance.

At the top, Dortmunder shook out the coil of rope,
holding on to the end tied to the metal hook. The rope
was knotted every few feet and dangled to about eight
feet from the ground. Dortmunder attached it to the top
of the wall with the hook and tugged it to be sure it was
solid. It was.

As soon as the searchlight glided by the next time,
Dortmunder zipped up the rest of the ladder and straddled the top of the wall just to the right. Chefwick hurried up after him, hampered slightly by the black bag,
and straddled the wall just to the left, facing Dortmunder.
They reached down, grabbed the ladder by the top rung,
pulled it up until it would tilt over the wall, and then
slid it down the other side. About nine feet down was a
flat tar roof, over the prison laundry. The ladder touched
the roof and Dortmunder immediately clambered onto
it. He took the black bag from Chefwick and hurried
down the ladder. Chefwick scrambled down after him.
They put the ladder down next to the low wall that edged
the roof and then lay down on top of the ladder, where
they would be in that wall's shadow the next time the
searchlight came by.

Outside, Kelp had been standing beside the truck,
squinting to see Dortmunder and Chefwick and the ladder. He saw them vaguely, huddled on the ladder, one
time when the searchlight went by on the other side of
the wall, but the next time it went by they were gone.

He nodded in satisfaction, got into the cab, and drove away from there, lights still off.

Dortmunder and Chefwick, meantime, used the ladder to get from the laundry roof to the ground. They put the ladder on the ground to one side and hurried for the main prison building looming up in the darkness ahead of them. They had to duck behind a wall once, to let the searchlight go by, but then trotted on, got to the building, found the door where it was supposed to be, and Chefwick took from his pocket the two tools he'd known he would have to use on this door. He went to work while Dortmunder kept watch.

Dortmunder saw the searchlight coming again, running along the face of the building. "Hurry it up," he whispered, and heard a click, and turned to see the door opening.

They ducked inside, shut the door, and the searchlight went by. "Close," Dortmunder whispered.

"I'll take my bag now," Chefwick whispered back. He was completely unruffled.

The room they were in was totally black, but Chefwick knew the contents of his bag so well he didn't need light. He squatted on the floor, opened the bag, put the two tools away in their appropriate pouches, took out two others, closed the bag, stood, and said, "All right."

Several locked doors away, Greenwood was saying, "I'll come quietly. Don't you worry, I'll come quietly."

"We're not worried," one of the guards said.

It had taken them all quite a while to get everything sorted out. After Greenwood had suddenly gotten calm the guards had tried to find out what had happened, what it was all about, but all the old man could do was sputter and point, and all Greenwood would do was stand around looking vague and shaking his head and saying, "I just don't know any more." Then the old man said the magic word "feet" and Greenwood erupted again.

He was very careful about how he erupted. He did nothing physical, all he did was scream and shout and thrash a bit. He kept it up while the guards held on to his arms, but when he saw they were about deciding to apply a local anesthetic to his head he calmed down again and became very reasonable. He explained about the old man's feet, being totally lucid, explaining to them as though he thought once they understood the situation they would thoroughly agree with him.

What they did was humor him, and that was what he wanted. And when one of them said, "Look, fellow, why don't we just find you someplace else to sleep?" Greenwood smiled in honest pleasure. He knew where they would take him now, to one of the cells over in the hospital wing. He could cool off there until morning, and then be handy for the doctor to see.

That's what they thought.

Greenwood said a smiling goodbye to the old man, who was holding a sock to his bleeding nose now, and out he marched amid the guards. He assured them he would go with them quietly and they assured him they weren't worried about that.

The early part of the route was the same as when he'd gone to see Prosker. Down the metal corridor, down the metal spiral stairs, along the other metal corridor and through two doors, both of which had to be unlocked by people on the outside and both of which were locked again in his wake. After that the route changed, going down a long brown corridor and around a corner to a nice lonely spot where two men dressed all in black, with black hoods over their heads and black pistols in their hands, came out of a doorway and said, "Don't nobody make a sound."

The guards looked at Dortmunder and Chefwick, for indeed it was they, and blinked in astonishment. One of them said, "You're crazy."

"Not necessarily," Chefwick said. He stepped to one side of the doorway and said, "In here, gentlemen."

"You won't shoot," the second guard said. "The noise would attract a lot of attention."

"That's why we have silencers," Dortmunder told him. "That's this thing like a hand grenade on the front of the gun. Want to hear it?"

"No," said the guard.

Everybody went into the room and Greenwood shut the door. They used the guards' belts to tie their ankles, their ties to tie their hands, and their shirttails to gag them. The room they were in was small and square and was somebody's office, with a metal desk. There was a phone on the desk but Dortmunder ripped the cord loose.

When they left the office, Chefwick carefully locked the door behind him. Dortmunder said to Greenwood, "This way," and the three of them loped down a corridor and through a heavy metal door that had been locked for several years until Chefwick had gotten to it. As Chefwick had said the other day, "Locks in prisons are meant to keep people in, not out. The outsides of the doors are much easier, that's where all the bolts and chains and machinery are."

They retraced the route that Dortmunder and Chefwick had taken coming in here. Four more doors stood in the way, each having been unlocked by Chefwick on the way in and each now being locked again on their way out. They came at last to the exit from this building and waited there, clustered around the doorway, looking at the black cube of the laundry across the way. Dortmunder checked his watch and it was three-twenty. "Five minutes," he whispered.

Four blocks away, Kelp looked at his watch, saw it was three-twenty, and got out of the truck cab again. He was finally getting used to the fact that the interior light didn't go on when he opened the door, he having removed the bulb himself before they left the city. He closed the door quietly, went around back, and opened the rear doors. "Set," he whispered to Murch.

"Right," Murch whispered back and began pushing a long one-by-twelve board out of the truck. Kelp grabbed the end of it and lowered it to the ground so the board leaned against the rear edge of the truck body in a long slant. Murch pushed out another board and Kelp lined it up beside the other one, with a space of about five feet between the two.

They had chosen the most industrial area of Utopia Park for this part of the plot. The streets directly contiguous with the prison were all shabby residential, but starting two or three blocks out the neighborhoods began to change. To the north and east were residential neighborhoods, steadily improving the farther away they got, and to the west was a poorer residential area that got progressively slummier till it petered out in a flurry of used car lots, but to the south was Utopia Park's industry. For block after block there was nothing but the low brick buildings in which sunglasses were made, soft drinks were bottled, tires were recapped, newspapers were printed, dresses were sewn, signs were painted, and foam rubber was covered with fabric. There was no traffic here at night, there were no pedestrians, a police car prowled through only once an hour. There was nothing here at night but all the factories and, parked in front of them, hundreds of trucks. Up this street and down that, nothing but trucks, bumpy-fendered, big-nosed, hulking, dark, empty, silent. Trucks.

Kelp had parked his truck in with all the other trucks, making it invisible. He had parked just beyond a fire hydrant so there would be room behind the truck, but other than that one open space the rest of the block was pretty well full. Kelp had had to drive around half a dozen blocks before he'd found this space, and it pleased him.

Now, with the two boards slanting out from the truck to the street, Kelp stepped up on the curb and waited. Murch had disappeared into the blackness inside the truck again, and after a minute there was the sudden chatter of an engine starting up in there. It roared a brief second, then settled down to a quiet purr, and out from the truck nosed a nearly new dark green Mercedes-Benz 250SE convertible. Kelp had run across it earlier this evening on Park Avenue in the Sixties. Because it wasn't going to be used very much, it still bore its MD plates. Kelp had decided to forgive doctors.

The boards bowed beneath the weight of the car. Murch, behind the wheel, looked like Gary Cooper taxiing his Grumman into position on the aircraft carrier. Nodding at Kelp the way Coop used to nod at the ground crew, Murch tapped the accelerator and the Mercedes-Benz went away, lights out.

Murch had spent some of his idle time in the back of the truck reading the owner's manual he'd found in the car's glove compartment, and he wondered if the top speed of one hundred eighteen miles an hour was on the up and up or not. He shouldn't test it now, but coming back maybe he'd have enough of a straightaway to find out.

Back in the prison, Dortmunder had checked his watch again, found that five minutes had passed, and said, "Okay." Now the three of them were trotting across the open space toward the laundry, the searchlight having flashed by just before they started.

Dortmunder and Chefwick put up the ladder and Greenwood led the way up it. The three got to the roof, pulled the ladder up after them, lay down in the lee of the low perimeter wall, held their breaths while the searchlight went by, and then got to their feet and carried the ladder over to the outer wall. Chefwick went up first this time, toting his black bag, went over the top, and went down the rope hand over hand, the handle of the black bag clamped in his teeth. Greenwood followed him and Dortmunder came last. Dortmunder straddled the top of the wall and began pulling the ladder up. The searchlight was coming back.

Chefwick dropped to the ground just as Murch arrived in the convertible. Chefwick took the bag from his teeth, which were aching from the strain, and climbed over the side into the convertible. The interior lights of this vehicle hadn't been tampered with, so they couldn't open the door.

Greenwood was coming down the rope. Dortmunder was still pulling up the ladder. The searchlight reached him, washed over him like magic water, passed on, stopped dead, quivered, and shot back. Dortmunder was gone, but the ladder was in the process of falling onto the laundry roof. It went *chack* when it hit.

Meantime, Greenwood had reached the ground and jumped into the front seat of the convertible, Chefwick being already in back. Dortmunder was coming very fast down the rope.

A siren said, *Rrrrrr*—and began its climb.

Dortmunder kicked out from the wall, let go the rope, dropped into the back seat of the convertible and called, "Go!"

Murch hit the accelerator.

Sirens were starting up all over the place. Kelp, standing by the truck with an unlit flashlight in his hands, began to chew his lower lip.

Murch had turned on the headlights, since he was going too fast now to depend on the occasional street lights. Behind them, the prison was coming to life like a yellow volcano. Any minute it would start erupting police cars.

Murch made a left on two wheels. He now had a three-block straightaway. He put the accelerator on the floor.

There are still milkmen who get up very early in the morning and deliver milk. One of these, standing at his steering wheel, put-putted his stubby white traveling walk-in closet into the middle of an intersection, looked to his left, and saw headlights coming at him too fast to think about. He yipped and threw himself backward into his cases of milk, causing a lot of crashing.

Murch went around the stalled milk truck like a skier on a slalom, and kept the accelerator on the floor. He was going to have to brake soon, and the speedometer hadn't broken a hundred yet.

No good. He'd have to brake now, or overshoot. He released the accelerator and tapped the brakes. Four-wheel disc brakes grabbed and held.

Kelp didn't hear the engine over the screaming sirens, but he did hear the tires shriek. He looked down at the corner and the convertible slid sideways into view, then leaped forward like Jim Brown going around end.

Kelp switched on his flashlight and began madly to wave it. Didn't Murch see him? The convertible kept getting larger.

Murch knew what he was doing. While his passengers clung to the upholstery and each other he shot down the block, tapped the brakes just enough at the right split second, nudged the wheel just enough, rolled up the boards and into the truck, tapped the brakes again, and came to a quivering standstill two inches from the far wall. He shut off the engine and switched off the lights.

Kelp, meanwhile, had put away his flashlight and was quickly shoving the boards back into the truck. He slammed one of the doors, hands reached down to help him up into the truck, and then the other door was shut.

For half a minute there was no sound in the blackness inside the truck except five people panting. Then Greenwood said, "We've gotta go back. I forgot my toothbrush."

Everybody laughed at that, but it was just nervous laughter. Still, it helped to relax them all. Murch turned the car's headlights on again, since they'd already proved no light from in here could be seen outside the truck, and then everybody shook hands with everybody, congratulating everybody on a job well done.

They got quiet and listened as a police car yowled by, and then Kelp said, "Hot on our trail," and everybody grinned again.

They'd done it. From here on it was simple. They'd wait here in the truck till around six, and then Kelp would slip out, get into the cab, and drive them all away from here. It was unlikely he'd be stopped, but if he was he was perfectly safe. He had legitimate papers for the rental truck, legitimate-looking driver's license and other identification, and a legitimate-sounding reason for being abroad. In a quiet spot in Brooklyn the convertible would be removed from the truck and left with its keys in it invitingly close to a vocational high school. The truck would be driven to Manhattan and left at the garage where Major Iko's man would pick it up and return it to the rental agency.

Everybody was feeling pleased and happy and relieved. They sat around in the convertible and told jokes and after a while Kelp brought out a deck of cards and they started to play poker for high paper stakes.

Along about four o'clock Kelp said, "Well, tomorrow we go get the emerald and collect our dough."

Greenwood said, "We can start working on it tomorrow, I guess. Three cards," he said to Chefwick, who was dealing jacks or better.

Everybody got very quiet. Dortmunder said to Greenwood, "What do you mean, we can start working on it?"

Greenwood gave a nervous shrug. "Well, it isn't going to be all that easy," he said.

Dortmunder said, "Why not?"

Greenwood cleared his throat. He looked around with an embarrassed smile. "Because," he said, "I hid it in the police station."

PHASE THREE

PHASE
THREE

1

Major Iko said, "In the police station?" He stared at everybody in blank disbelief.

They were all there, all five of them. Dortmunder and Kelp, sitting in their usual places in front of his desk. Greenwood, the one they'd gotten out of prison last night, sitting between them in a chair he'd pulled over from the wall. And two new ones, introduced as Roger Chefwick and Stan Murch. A part of Major Iko's mind was fondling those two new names, could hardly wait for this meeting to be over so he could give the orders for two new dossiers to be made up.

But the rest of his mind, the major portion of the Major's mind, was given over to incredulity. He stared at everyone, and most especially at Greenwood. "In the police station?" he said, and his voice cracked.

"It's where I was," Greenwood said reasonably.

"But surely—at the Coliseum you could have—somewhere—"

"He swallowed it," Dortmunder said.

The Major looked at Dortmunder, trying to understand what the man had just said. "I beg your pardon?"

It was Greenwood who answered. "When I saw they were going to get me," he said, "I was in a hall. No place to hide anything. Couldn't even throw it away. I didn't want them to find it on me, so I swallowed it."

"I see," the Major said, a bit shakily, and then smiled a thin smile and said, "It's a good thing for you I'm an atheist, Mr. Greenwood."

In polite bafflement, Greenwood said, "It is?"

"The original significance of the Balabomo Emerald in my tribe was religious," the Major said. "Go on with your story. When did you next see the emerald?"

"Not till the next day," Greenwood said. "I'll sort of skip over that part, if you don't mind."

"I wish you would."

"Right. When I had the emerald again, I was in a cell. I guess they were afraid the rest of the guys might try to spring me right away, 'cause they hid me out in a precinct on the Upper West Side for the first two days. I was in one of the detention cells on the top floor."

"And that's where you hid it?" the Major said faintly.

"There wasn't anything else I could do, Major. I didn't dare keep it on my person, not in jail."

"Couldn't you have just kept on swallowing it?"

Greenwood gave a greenish smile. "Not after the first time I got it back," he said.

"Mm-mm," the Major admitted reluctantly. He looked at Dortmunder.

"Well? What now?"

Dortmunder said, "We're divided. Two for, two against, and one uncertain."

"You mean, whether or not to go after the emerald again?"

"Right."

"But—" The Major spread his hands. "Why wouldn't you go after it? If you've successfully broken into a prison, surely an ordinary precinct house—"

"That's just it," Dortmunder said. "My feeling is we're pushing our luck. We've given you two capers for the price of one as it is. We can't just keep busting into places forever. Sooner or later the odds have to catch up with us."

The Major said, "Odds? Luck? But it isn't odds and luck that have helped you, Mr. Dortmunder, it's skill and planning and experience. You still have just as much skill and are capable of just as much planning as in last night's affair, and now you have even more experience."

"I just have a feeling," Dortmunder said. "This is turning into one of those dreams where you keep running down the same corridor and you never get anywhere."

"But surely if Mr. Greenwood hid the emerald, and knows where he hid it, and—" The Major looked at Greenwood. "It is hidden well, is it not?"

"It's hidden well," Greenwood assured him. "It'll still be there."

The Major spread his hands. "Then I don't see the problem. Mr. Dortmunder, I take it you are one of the two opposed."

"That's right," Dortmunder said. "Chefwick is with

me. Greenwood wants to go after it, and Kelp is on his side. Murch doesn't know."

"I'll go along with the majority," Murch said. "I got no opinion."

Chefwick said, "My opposition is similarly based to Dortmunder's. I believe one can reach the point where one is throwing good expertise after bad, and I fear we have reached that point."

Greenwood said to Chefwick, "It's a cinch. I tell you, it's a precinct house. You know what that means, the joint is full of guys typing. The last thing they'll expect is somebody breaking in. It'll be easier than the jug you just got me out of."

"Besides," Kelp said, also talking to Chefwick, "we've worked at the damn thing this long, I hate to give it up."

"I understand that," Chefwick said, "and in some ways I sympathize with it. But at the same time I do feel the mathematical pressure of the odds against us. We have performed two operations now, and none of us is dead, none of us is in jail, none of us is even wounded. Only Greenwood has had his cover blown, and being a single man with no dependents, it won't be at all hard for him to rebuild. I believe we should consider ourselves very lucky to have done as well as we have, and I believe we should retire and consider some other job somewhere else."

"Say," said Kelp, "that's just the point. We're still all of us on our uppers, we've still got to find a caper somewhere to get us squared away. We know about this emerald, why not go after it?"

Dortmunder said, "Three jobs for the price of one?"

The Major said, "You're right about that, Mr. Dort-munder. You are doing more work than you contracted for, and you should be paid more. Instead of the thirty thousand dollars a man we originally agreed to, we'll make it—" The Major paused, thinking, then said, "Thirty-two thousand. An extra ten thousand to be split among you."

Dortmunder snorted. "Two thousand dollars to break into a police station? I wouldn't break into a tollbooth for money like that."

Kelp looked at the Major with the expression of a man disappointed in an old friend and protégé. "That's awful little, Major," he said. "If that's the kind of offer you're going to make, you shouldn't say anything at all."

The Major frowned, looking from face to face. "I don't know what to say," he admitted.

"Say ten thousand," Kelp told him.

"A man?"

"That's right. And the weekly amount up to two hun-dred."

The Major considered. But too quick an agreement might make them suspicious, so he said, "I couldn't make it that much. My country couldn't afford it, we're strain-ing the national budget as it is."

"How much, then?" Kelp asked him in a friendly, helpful sort of way.

The Major drummed fingertips on the desktop. He squinted, he closed one eye, he scratched his head above his left ear. Finally he said, "Five thousand."

"And the two hundred a week."

The Major nodded. "Yes."

Kelp looked at Dortmunder. "Sweet enough?" he asked.

Dortmunder chewed a knuckle, and it occurred to the Major to wonder if Dortmunder too was padding his part. But then Dortmunder said, "I'll look it over. If it looks good to me, and if it looks good to Chefwick, all right."

"Naturally," the Major said, "the pay will continue while you look things over."

"Naturally," Dortmunder said.

They all got to their feet. The Major said to Greenwood, "May I offer you congratulations, by the way, on your freedom."

"Thanks," Greenwood said. "You wouldn't know where I could find an apartment, do you? Two and a half or three, moderately priced, in a good neighborhood?"

"I'm sorry," the Major said.

"If you hear of anything," Greenwood said, "let me know."

"I will," said the Major.

2

Murch, obviously very drunk and holding a nearly empty pint of Old Mr. Boston apricot brandy in his hand, stepped off the curb, out in front of the police car, waggled his other hand at it, and cried, "Takshi!"

The police car stopped. It was that or run over him. Murch leaned on the fender and announced loudly, "I wanna go home. Brooklyn. Take me to Brooklyn, cabby, and be fast about it." It was well after midnight and except for Murch this residential block on Manhattan's Upper West Side was quiet and peaceful.

The non-driving policeman got out of the police car. He said, "Comere, you."

Murch staggered over. Winking hugely he said, "Never mind the meter, pal. We can work out a private arrangement. The cops'll never know."

"Izzat right?" said the cop.

"That's only one of the million things the cops don't know," Murch confided.

"Oh, yeah?" The cop opened the rear door. "Climb aboard, chum," he said.

"Right," said Murch. He lurched into the police car and fell asleep at once on the rear seat.

The cops didn't take Murch to Brooklyn. They took him to the precinct house, where they woke him without gentleness, took him from the back seat of their car, trotted him up the slate steps between the green lights—the globe on the left one was broken—and turned him over to some other cops on the inside. "Let him sleep it off in the tank," one of them commented.

There was a brief ritual at the desk, and then the new cops trotted Murch down a long green corridor and shoved him into the tank, which was a big square metal room full of bars and drunks. "This isn't right," Murch told himself, and he began to shout. "Yo! Hey! What the hey! Son of a bitch!"

All the other drunks had been trying to sleep it off like they were supposed to, and Murch doing all that shouting woke them up and irritated them. "Shut up, bo," one of them said.

"Oh, yeah?" Murch said and hit him in the mouth, and pretty soon there was a good fight going on in the drunk tank. Most people missed when they swung, but at least they were swinging.

The cell door opened and some cops came in, saying, "Break it up." They broke it up, and worked it out that Murch was the cause of the trouble. "I ain't staying here with these bums," Murch announced, and the cops said, "Indeed you aren't, brother."

They took Murch out of the drunk tank, being not

at all gentle with him, and ran him very rapidly up four flights of stairs to the fifth and top floor of the precinct, where the detention cells were.

Murch was hoping for the second cell on the right, because if he got the second cell on the right that was the end of the problem. Unfortunately, there was somebody else already in the second cell on the right, and Murch wound up in the fourth cell on the left. They pushed him in at high speed and shut the door behind him. Then they went away.

There was light, not much, coming from the end of the corridor. Murch sat down on the blanket-covered metal bunk and opened his shirt. Inside, taped to his chest, were some sheets of typewriter paper and a ballpoint pen. He removed these from his chest, wincing, and then made a lot of diagrams and notes while it was still fresh in his mind. Then he taped it all back to his chest again, lay down on the metal bunk, and went to sleep.

In the morning he was given a good talking to, but because he had no record and he apologized and was very chagrined and embarrassed and decent about it all, he was not held.

Outside, Murch looked across the street and saw a two-year-old Chrysler with MD plates. He went over and Kelp was behind the wheel, taking photographs of the front of the station house. Chefwick was in the back seat, keeping a head count on people going in and coming out, cars going in and coming out at the driveway beside the building, things like that.

Murch got into the Chrysler beside Kelp, who said, "Hi."

"Hi," Murch said. "Boy, don't ever be a drunk. Cops are death on drunks."

A little later, when they were done, Kelp and Chefwick drove Murch across town to where his Mustang was parked. "Somebody stole your hubcaps," Kelp said.

"I take them off when I come to Manhattan," Murch said. "Manhattan is full of thieves." He opened his shirt, removed the papers from his chest again, and gave them to Kelp. Then he got in his car and drove home. He went up to 125th Street and over to the Triborough Bridge and around Grand Central Parkway to Van Wyck Expressway to the Belt Parkway and home that way. It was a hot day, full of sun and humidity, so when he got home he took a shower and then went downstairs to his bedroom and lay on the bed in his underwear and read what Cahill had to say about the Chevy Camaro.

3

This time the ebony man with the long thin fingers took Kelp to the room with the pool table right away, without detours or side trips. He bowed his head slightly at Kelp and left, closing the door behind him.

It was a hot night outside, the last week in July, humidity building up toward 1,000 percent. Kelp was in thin slacks and a short-sleeved white shirt and the central air conditioning in here was making him chilly. He wiped leftover perspiration from his forehead, lifted his arms to air his underarms, walked over to the pool table, and racked up the balls.

He didn't feel like much of anything tonight, so he just practiced breaks. He'd rack the balls, line the cue ball up in this spot or in that spot, hit it here or there with or without some kind of english, aim for one spot or another spot on the lead ball, and see what would happen. Then he'd rack them again, set the cue ball up somewhere else, and do it all over again.

When the Major came in he said, "You haven't progressed so far tonight."

"Just fooling around this time," Kelp told him. He put the cue down and took a damp and crumpled sheet of paper from his hip pocket. He unfolded it and handed it over to Iko, who took it with some apparent reluctance to have his fingers touch it. Kelp turned back to the table, where he'd just made a break that had dropped two balls, and began to sink the rest of them, quickly but methodically.

He'd put three away when Iko squeaked, "A helicopter?"

Kelp put the cue down and turned back to say, "We weren't sure you could get your hands on one of those, but if you can't we don't have any caper. So Dortmunder said I should just bring you the list like always and let you decide for yourself."

Iko was looking a little strange. "A helicopter," he said. "How do you expect me to get you a helicopter?"

Kelp shrugged. "I dunno. But the way we figured, you've got a whole country behind you."

"That's true," Iko said, "but the country behind me is Talabwo, it is not the United States."

Kelp said, "Talabwo doesn't have any helicopters?"

"Of course Talabwo has helicopters," Iko said irritably. It looked as though his national pride was stung. "We have seven helicopters. But they are in Talabwo, naturally, and Talabwo is in Africa. The American authorities might ask questions if we tried to import an American helicopter from Talabwo."

"Yeah," Kelp said. "Let me think," he said.

"There's nothing else on this list to cause any trouble," Iko said. "Are you sure you have to have a helicopter?"

"The detention cells," Kelp said, "are on the top floor, which is the fifth floor. You go in the street entrance, you've got five floors of armed cops to go through before you ever reach the cells, and then you've got the same five floors of cops to go through all over again before you get back to the street. And you know what's out on the street?"

Iko shook his head.

"Cops," Kelp told him. "Usually three or four prowl cars, plus cops walking around, going in, coming out, maybe just standing around on the sidewalk, talking to each other."

"I see," said Iko.

"So our only chance," Kelp told him, "is to come down from the top. Get on the roof, and go from there down into the building. Then the detention cells are right there, handy, and we don't even see most of the cops. And after we get the emerald we don't have to fight our way through anybody, all we have to do is go back up to the roof and take off."

"I see," said Iko.

Kelp picked up his cue, dropped the seven, walked around the table.

Iko said, "But a helicopter is very loud. They'll hear you coming."

"No, they won't," Kelp said. He leaned over the table, dropped the four, straightened, said, "There's airplanes going over that neighborhood all day long. Big jets landing at LaGuardia, they go over that neighborhood a lot lower than you'd think. You know, they start their approach, some of them, like out at Allentown."

"You'll use their noise to help you?"

"We've kept a record on them," Kelp said. "We know who the regulars are, and we'll drift in while one of them is going by." He sank the twelve.

Iko said, "What if someone sees you, from some other building? There are taller buildings around there, aren't there?"

"They see a helicopter land on a police station roof," Kelp said. "So what?" He dropped the six.

"All right," Iko said. "I can see where it could work."

"And nothing else can work for a minute," Kelp told him and dropped the fifteen.

"Perhaps," Iko said. He frowned in a troubled way. "You could be right. But the problem is, where am I going to get you a helicopter?"

"I don't know," Kelp said, sinking the two. "Where'd you get your helicopters before this?"

"Well, we bought them, naturally, from—" Iko stopped, and his eyes widened. A white cloud formed above his head, and in the cloud a lightbulb appeared. The lightbulb flashed on. "I *can* do it!" he cried.

Kelp dropped the eleven and, on ricochet, the eight. That left the three and the fourteen still around. "Good," he said and put the cue down. "How you going to manage it?"

"We'll simply order a helicopter," Iko said, "through normal channels. I can arrange that. When it arrives in Newark for transshipment by boat to Talabwo, it will spend a few days in our warehouse space. I can arrange for you to be able to borrow it, but not during normal working hours."

"We wouldn't want it during normal working hours," Kelp told him. "About seven-thirty in the evening is when we figure to get there."

"That will be fine, then," the Major said. He was obviously delighted with himself. "I will have it gassed up and ready," he said.

"Fine."

"The only thing is," the Major said, his delight fading just a trifle, "it could take a while for the order to go through. Three weeks, possibly longer."

"That's okay," Kelp said. "The emerald will keep. Just so we get our salary every week."

"I'll get it as quickly as I can," Iko said.

Kelp motioned at the table. "Mind?"

"Go ahead," Iko said. He watched Kelp sink the last two and then said, "Perhaps I ought to take lessons in that. It does look relaxing."

"You don't need lessons," Kelp told him. "Just grab a cue and start shooting. It'll come to you. Want me to show you how?"

The Major looked at his watch, obviously torn two ways. "Well," he said, "just for a few minutes."

4

Dortmunder was sorting money on his coffee table, a little pile of crumpled singles, a smaller pile of less-crumpled fives, and a thin pair of tens. His shoes and socks were off and he kept wiggling his toes as though they'd just been released from prison. It was late evening, the long August day finally coming to an end outside the window, and Dortmunder's loosened tie, rumpled shirt, and matted hair demonstrated he hadn't spent much of that day here in his air-conditioned apartment.

The doorbell rang.

Dortmunder got heavily to his feet, went over to the door, and peered through the spy hole. Kelp's cheerful face was framed there, as in a cameo. Dortmunder opened the door and Kelp came in, saying, "Well, how's it going?"

Dortmunder shut the door. "You look pleased with life," he said.

"I am," Kelp said. "Why not?" He glanced at the

money on the coffee table. "You don't seem to be doing too bad yourself."

Dortmunder limped back to the sofa and sat down. "You don't think so? Out all day, walking from door to door, chased by dogs, jeered at by children, insulted by housewives, and what do I get for it?" He made a contemptuous wave at the money on the coffee table. "Seventy bucks," he said.

"It's the heat that's slowing you down," Kelp told him. "You want a drink?"

"It isn't the heat," Dortmunder said, "it's the humidity. Yeah, I want a drink."

Kelp went to the kitchenette and talked from there, saying, "What sort of dodge you working?"

"Encyclopedias," Dortmunder said. "And the problem is, you ask for more than a ten-buck deposit they either balk or they want to write a check. As it is, I got one ten-dollar check today, and what the hell am I going to do with that?"

"Blow your nose in it," Kelp suggested. He came out of the kitchen with two glasses containing bourbon and ice. "Why you doing the encyclopedias?" he asked.

Dortmunder nodded at the slender briefcase over by the door. "Because that's what I got the display case on," he said. "You can't sell a thing without a lot of bright pieces of paper."

Kelp handed him a glass and went over to sit down in the armchair. "I guess I'm luckier," he said. "Most of my work is done in bars."

"What are you up to?"

"Me and Greenwood are working the smack over by

Penn Station," Kelp said. "We split almost three hundred today."

Dortmunder looked at him in disbelief. "The smack? That still works?"

"They lap it up like cream," Kelp said. "And why wouldn't they? It's me and the mark against Greenwood, there's no way on earth we can lose. One of us has to win."

"I know," Dortmunder said. "I know all about it, I've tried that dodge myself once or twice, but I don't have the face for it. It needs cheerful types like you and Greenwood." He sipped at his bourbon and sat back on the sofa, closing his eyes and breathing through his mouth.

"Hell," Kelp said, "why not take it easy? You can make ends meet on Iko's two hundred."

"I want to build a stake," Dortmunder said, keeping his eyes closed. "I don't like living on the bone like this."

"That's a hell of a stake you'll build," Kelp told him, "at seventy bucks a day."

"Sixty yesterday," Dortmunder said. He opened his eyes. "We've been tapping Iko four weeks since Greenwood got out. How much longer you think he'll ante up?"

"Till he gets the helicopter," Kelp said.

"If he gets it. Maybe he won't get it at all. He didn't sound happy when he paid me last week." Dortmunder drank some bourbon. "And I'll tell you something else," he said. "I don't have the belief in this job I have in some things. I've got my eyes open for something else,

I've spread the word around I'm available. Anything else comes along, that rotten emerald can go to hell."

"That's the way I feel too," Kelp said. "That's why Greenwood and me are matching coins up and down Seventh Avenue. But I believe Iko's going to come through."

"I don't," Dortmunder said.

Kelp grinned. "You want to put a little side bet on it?"

Dortmunder looked at him. "Whyn't you call Greenwood over and I can bet you both?"

Kelp looked innocent. "Say, don't be in a bad mood," he said. "I'm just kidding with you."

Dortmunder emptied his glass. "I know it," he said. "Build me another?"

"Sure thing." Kelp came over and took Dortmunder's glass and the phone rang. "There's Iko now," Kelp said, grinning, and went out to the kitchenette.

Dortmunder answered the phone and Iko's voice said, "I have it."

"Well, I'll be damned," Dortmunder said.

5

The lavender Lincoln with the MD plates nosed slowly amid the long low warehouses on the Newark docks. The setting sun cast long shadows across the empty streets. Today was Tuesday, the fifteenth of August; the sun had risen at eleven minutes past five this morning and would set at two minutes before seven this evening. The time was now six-thirty.

Murch, who was driving, found the sun reflected into his eyes from the rearview mirror. He switched the mirror to the night setting, reducing the sun to a yellowish ball in an olive haze, and said irritably, "Where the hell is this place anyway?"

"Not much farther," Kelp said. He was holding the typed sheet of instructions in his hands and was sitting beside Murch. The other three were in back, Dortmunder on the right, Chefwick in the middle, Greenwood on the left. They were all in their guard uniforms again, the policelike costumes they'd worn at the Coliseum. Murch, who didn't have a uniform like that, was wearing a Greyhound bus driver's jacket and cap. Although it was properly hot for August outside, the air conditioning inside made it jacket-and-cap-wearing weather.

"Turn there," Kelp said, pointing ahead.

Murch shook his head in disgust. "Which way?" he said with studied patience.

"Left," Kelp said. "Didn't I say that?"

"Thank you," Murch said. "No, you didn't."

Murch turned left, into a narrow blacktop alley between two brick warehouses. It was already twilight in here, but sun shone orange on stacked wooden crates at the far end. Murch steered the Lincoln around the crates and out to a large open area surrounded on all sides by the backs of warehouses. The blacktop ran one lane wide along the rear of the warehouses, like a frame around a picture, but the picture itself was nothing but a big flat square of weedy dirt. In the middle of the empty space stood the helicopter.

"That's big," Kelp said. He sounded awed.

The helicopter looked huge, standing out there all alone like that. It was painted a dull Army brown, had a round glass nose, small glass side windows, and blades that hung out like washlines.

Murch jounced the Lincoln over the rough ground and stopped near the helicopter. Up close it didn't look as gigantic. They could see it was just a little taller than a man and not much longer than the Lincoln. Squares and rectangles of black tape covered the body here and there, apparently to hide identifying numbers or symbols.

They all got out of the cool Lincoln into the hot

world and Murch rubbed his hands together as he grinned at the machine in front of them. "Now, there's a baby that'll go," he said.

Dortmunder, suddenly suspicious, said, "You *did* drive one of these things before, right?"

"I told you," Murch said. "I can drive anything."

"Yeah," Dortmunder said. "That's what you told me, I remember that."

"Right," said Murch. He kept grinning at the helicopter.

"You *can* drive anything," Dortmunder said, "but the question is *did* you ever drive one of *these* things before?"

"Don't answer him," Kelp said to Murch. "I don't want to know the answer, and neither does he, not now. Come on, let's load up."

"Right," said Murch, while Dortmunder slowly shook his head. Murch went around and opened the Lincoln's trunk and they all started to carry things from the trunk over to the helicopter. Chefwick carried his black bag, Greenwood and Dortmunder carried the machine guns and between them toted by its handles a green metal box full of detonators and tear gas grenades and miscellaneous tools. Kelp carried a cardboard carton full of handcuffs and strips of white cloth. Murch checked to be sure the Lincoln was locked up tight, then followed carrying the portable jammer, a heavy black box about the size of a beer case, bristling with knobs and dials and retracted antennas.

The inside of the helicopter was similar to the inside of a car, with two padded bucket seats up front and a long seat across the back. There was stowage space behind the back seat into which they shoved everything, then arranged themselves with Murch at the wheel, Dortmunder beside him, and the other three in back. They shut the door and Dortmunder studied Murch studying the controls. After a minute Dortmunder said in disgust, "You never even *saw* one of these things before."

Murch turned on him. "Are you kidding? I read in *Popular Mechanics* how to *make* one, you don't think I can *drive* one?"

Dortmunder looked over his shoulder at Kelp. "I could be peddling encyclopedias right now," he said.

Murch, having been insulted, said to Dortmunder, "Come on, now, watch this. I hit this switch here, see? And this lever. And I do this."

A roaring started. Dortmunder looked up, and through the glass bubble he could see the blades rotating. They went faster and faster and became a blur.

Murch tapped Dortmunder's knee. He was still explaining things as he did this and that to the controls, even though Dortmunder couldn't hear him any more. But Dortmunder kept watching, because anything was better than looking up at the noisy blur overhead.

Abruptly, Murch smiled and sat back and nodded and pointed out. Dortmunder looked out and the ground wasn't there. He leaned forward, looking through the bubble, and the ground was way down below, orange-yellow-green-black, jagged with long shadows from the setting sun. "Oh, yeah," Dortmunder said softly, though no one could hear him. "That's right."

Murch fiddled around for a couple of minutes, getting used to things, making the helicopter do some odd maneuvers, but then he settled down and they began to move northeast.

Dortmunder had never realized before just how full the sky was. Newark Airport was just a little ways behind them, and the sky was as full of circling planes as a shopping center parking lot on a Saturday is full of people circling to find a place to park. Murch was moving along under them, heading for New York at a good clip. They passed over Newark Bay and Jersey City and Upper Bay and then Murch figured out how to steer and he turned left a little and they followed the Hudson north, Manhattan on their right like stalagmites with cavities, New Jersey on their left like uncollected garbage.

After the first few minutes, Dortmunder liked it. Murch didn't seem to be doing anything wrong, and aside from the noise it was kind of nice to be hanging up in the sky here like this. The guys in back were nudging each other and pointing at things like the Empire State Building, and Dortmunder turned at one point and grinned at Kelp, who shrugged and grinned back.

The jet they were planning to use for cover normally roared over the police station at seven thirty-two every evening. Tonight they wouldn't be able to hear it, not being able to hear anything but themselves, so they would either have to see it or just take a chance on its being there. Dortmunder hadn't realized noise would be a problem like this, and it troubled him, detracting from the enjoyment of the ride.

Murch tapped him on the knee and pointed to the right. Dortmunder looked, and over there was another helicopter, with a radio station's call letters on the side. The pilot waved, and Dortmunder waved back. The man beside the pilot was too busy to wave, talking into a microphone and looking down at the West Side Highway, which was all snarled up.

Far away on their left the sun was sinking slowly into Pennsylvania, the sky turning pink and mauve and purple. Manhattan was already in twilight.

Dortmunder checked his watch. Seven-twenty. They were doing well.

The plan was to circle around the police station and come at it from the rear, so the cops out front wouldn't get a glimpse of the helicopter landing on their roof. Murch kept following the Hudson north, therefore, until Harlem stood snaggle-toothed on their right, and then he made a wide sweeping U-turn. It was like being a kid on one of those Coney Island rides, only higher up.

Murch had figured out the altitude adjustment by now. He eased down through the air over the Upper West Side, figuring out the street they wanted from landmarks like Central Park and the meeting of Broadway with West End Avenue. And then, dead ahead, there stood the black rectangle of the police station roof.

Kelp leaned forward and tapped Dortmunder's shoulder. When Dortmunder looked at him, he pointed to the sky on their right. Dortmunder looked up there and saw the jet coming out of the west, sweep-winged, sparkling, noisy. Dortmunder grinned and nodded.

Murch put it down on the roof as gently as he'd put a beer glass on a bar. He cut the engine and in their own sudden silence they could hear the passage of the jet, sliding down the sky above them toward LaGuardia.

"Last stop," Murch said, and the jet noise faded away to the east.

Dortmunder opened the door and they all clambered out. Chefwick hurried over to the door in the small shack-like construction atop the roof while the others unloaded the helicopter. Kelp took a pair of cable shears, went over to the front left edge of the roof, lay down on his belly, reached down and out, and cut the phone wires. Murch set the portable jammer down on the roof, turned it on, put earphones on, and began twiddling with the dials. All radio broadcasting from this building promptly became unintelligible.

By now Chefwick had the door open. Dortmunder and Greenwood had stuffed their pockets with detona-tors and tear gas grenades, and they followed Chefwick down the stairs to the windowless metal door at the bot-tom. Chefwick studied this door a second, then said, "I'll have to blast this one. Go on back up."

Kelp was on the way down, carrying the cardboard carton of handcuffs and strips of white cloth. Dortmunder met him midway and said, "Back up on the roof. Chefwick has to blast."

"Right."

The three of them hurried up to the roof, where Murch had left the jammer and was sitting on the roof near the front edge, several detonator caps beside him. He looked over at them and waved. Dortmunder showed him two fingers, meaning he should wait two minutes, and Murch nodded.

Chefwick came upstairs. Dortmunder said to him, "How we doing?"

"Three," Chefwick said in a distracted sort of way. "Two. One."

Phoom, said a noise.

Grayish smoke drifted lazily up the stairwell and out the door.

Dortmunder dashed downstairs through the smoke, found the metal door lying on its back at the bottom, and hurried through the doorway into a short square hall. Straight ahead, heavy barred gates blocked the end of the hall where the stairway went down. An astonished-looking cop was sitting on a high stool there, just inside the gates, with a paper-filled lectern beside him. He was a thin and elderly white-haired cop, and his reflexes were a little slow. Also, he wasn't armed. Dortmunder knew, from both Greenwood and Murch, that none of the cops on duty up here were armed.

"Take him," Dortmunder said over his shoulder and turned the other way, where a stout cop with a ham and cheese sandwich on rye in his hand was trying to close another gate. Dortmunder pointed the machine gun conversationally and said, "Stop that."

The cop looked at Dortmunder. He stopped and put his hands up in the air. One slice of rye dangled over his knuckles like the floppy ear of a dog.

Greenwood meanwhile had convinced the elderly cop to contemplate his retirement. The cop was standing beside his lectern with his hands up while Greenwood tossed three detonator caps and two tear gas grenades through the bars and down the stairs, where they made a mess. The idea was that no one was supposed to come upstairs.

There was one more officer on duty up here. He'd been in the area between the second gate and yet a third, where there was a scarred wooden desk. He'd been sitting at this desk, reading *Ramparts,* and when Dortmunder and Greenwood led the other two cops in at machine-gun point, the third one looked at them in bewilderment, put down his magazine, got to his feet, raised his hands over his head, and said, "You sure you got the right place?"

"Open up," Dortmunder said, gesturing at the last gate. Through there, in the detention block, arms could be seen waving through cell bars on both sides. Nobody in there knew what was going on exactly, but they all wanted to be a part of it.

"Brother," cop number three told Dortmunder, "the hardest case we got in there is a latvian sailor hit a bartender with a fifth of Johnny Walker Red Label. Seven stitches. You sure you want one of our people?"

"Just open," Dortmunder told him.

The cop shrugged. "Anything you say," he said.

Meanwhile, on the roof, Murch had started tossing detonator caps at the street. He wanted to make noise and confusion without killing anybody, which was easy the first couple of times he dropped the caps, but which became increasingly difficult as the street filled up with cops running around trying to figure out who was attacking who and from where.

In the precinct captain's office, on the second floor, the quiet evening had erupted into bedlam. The captain had gone home for the day, of course, the prisoners upstairs had been given their evening meal, the evening patrolman shift had been sent on its way, and the lieutenant in charge had been relaxing down into that slow quiet period of the day Dortmunder had been counting on. The lieutenant had been glancing through detectives' reports, in fact, looking for the dirty parts, when people started to run into his office.

The first one hadn't actually run, he'd walked. The patrolman on the switchboard it was, and he said, "Sir, the phone's gone dead."

"Oh? We'd better call the phone company to fix it pronto," the lieutenant said. He liked the word "pronto," it made him feel like Sean Connery. He reached for the phone to call the phone company, but when he held it to his ear there wasn't any sound.

He became aware of the patrolman looking at him. "Oh," he said. "Oh, yes." He put the phone back on its hook.

He was saved, momentarily, by the patrolman from the radio room, who came running in, looking bewildered, to say, "Sir, somebody's jamming our signal!"

"What?" The lieutenant had heard the words, but he hadn't comprehended their meaning.

"We can't broadcast," the patrolman said, "and we can't receive. Somebody's set up a jammer on us, I can tell, we used to have the same thing in the South Pacific."

"Something's broken," the lieutenant said. "That's all." He was worried, but he was damned if he was going to show it. "Something's just gotten broken, that's all."

There was an explosion somewhere in the building.

The lieutenant leaped to his feet. "My God! What was that?"

"An explosion, sir," the switchboard patrolman said. There was an explosion.

"Two explosions," the radio patrolman said. "Sir." There was a third explosion.

A patrolman ran in, shouting, "Bombs! In the street!"

The lieutenant took a quick step to the right, and then a quick step to the left. "Revolution," he babbled. "It's a revolution. They always go for the police stations first."

Another patrolman ran in, shouting, "Tear gas in the stairwell, sir! And somebody's blown up the stairs between the fourth and fifth floors!"

"Mobilize!" screamed the lieutenant. "Call the Governor! Call the Mayor!" He snatched up the phone. "Hello, hello! Emergency!"

Another patrolman ran in, shouting, "Sir, there's a fire in the street!"

"A what? A what?"

"A bomb hit a parked car. It's burning out there."

"Bombs? Bombs?" The lieutenant looked at the phone he was still holding, then flung it away as though it had grown teeth. "Break out the riot guns!" he shouted. "Get all personnel in the building to the first floor, on the double! I want a volunteer to carry a message through the enemy lines!"

"A message, sir? To whom?"

"To the phone company, who else? I've got to call the captain!"

Upstairs in the detention block, Kelp was using the handcuffs to lock cops' wrists behind their backs and the lengths of white cloth to gag them. Chefwick, having taken the keys to the cells from the desk, was unlocking the second cell on the right. Dortmunder and Greenwood were keeping alert, machine guns at the ready, and the clamor from all the other cells had increased to near pandemonium.

Inside the cell Chefwick was opening, staring out at them all with the blank astonished delight of someone whose most outlandish wish-fulfillment fantasy has just come true, was a short, wiry, bearded, dirty old man in a black raincoat, brown trousers, and gray sneakers. His hair was long and shaggy and gray, and so was his beard.

Chefwick opened the cell door. The old man said, "Me? Me, fellows?"

Greenwood went in, his machine gun carried casually in his left hand, and headed directly to the rear wall, brushing by the old man, who kept blinking at everybody and pointing at himself.

The side walls of the cell were metal and the front was composed of bars, but the rear wall, being the outer wall of the building, was stone. Greenwood stood on tiptoe, reached up to just under the ceiling, and plucked out a small piece of stone that didn't look any different from any other part of the wall. He then reached in behind where the stone had been.

Kelp and Dortmunder meantime had hustled the three cops into the detention block and were waiting just outside the cell to put the cops in there when Greenwood came out.

Greenwood, his fingers in the hole in the wall, looked around at Dortmunder and gave a very glassy smile.

Dortmunder went over to the cell doorway. "What's the matter?"

"I don't under—" Greenwood's fingers were scrabbling around in the hole like spiders. Faintly from outside they could hear detonator caps going off.

Dortmunder said, "It isn't there?"

The old man, looking from face to face, said, "Me, fellows?"

Greenwood looked at him in sudden suspicion. "You? Did you take it?"

The old man suddenly looked astonished in a fearful way. "Me? Me?"

"He didn't take it," Dortmunder said. "Look at him. He couldn't reach up there, for one thing."

Greenwood was beginning to get wild. "Who, then?" he said. "If not him, who?"

"The thing was there almost two months," Dortmunder said. He turned to Kelp. "Ungag one of them."

Kelp did so, and Dortmunder said to him, "When did this bird take occupancy?"

"Three A.M. this morning."

Greenwood said to Dortmunder, "I swear I put it—"

"I believe you," Dortmunder said. He sounded tired. "Somebody found it, that's all. Let's get out of here." He walked out of the cell, a troubled Greenwood coming frowning behind him.

The old man said, "What about me, fellows? You're takin' me along, ain'tcha, fellows?"

Dortmunder looked at him, then turned to the un-gagged cop and said, "What's he in for?"

"Exposing himself in Lord and Taylor."

"It's a frame-up!" cried the old man. "I never—"

"He's still in his working clothes," the cop said. "Have him open his raincoat."

The old man began to fuss and fidget. "That don't mean anything," he said.

Dortmunder said, "Open your raincoat."

"It don't mean a thing," the old man insisted.

"Open your raincoat," Dortmunder said.

The old man, hesitant, muttering, opened his rain-coat and spread it wide. Underneath, he wasn't wearing brown trousers at all. He was wearing cut-off trouser legs that extended up to just above the knee, where they were held on with garters. Above that, he wore nothing under the raincoat at all. He needed a bath.

Everybody looked at him. The old man giggled.

Dortmunder said, "Maybe you ought to stay here." He turned to the cops. "Go on in there with him."

The cops went in, Chefwick locked the door, and they left. There was no one at all at the head of the stairs, down past the last gate, but they tossed two more tear gas grenades down that way anyway. They hurried up the stairs to the roof, following the getaway plan just as though the Balabomo Emerald had been there where Greenwood left it, and at the top Dortmunder dropped three detonators down the stairwell and shut the door.

Murch was already in the helicopter, and when he saw them coming he started the engine. The rotors began to spin and roar, and Dortmunder and the others ran through the wind to the side of the helicopter and climbed in.

Down on the first floor, the lieutenant paused in his supervising of the handing out of riot guns to cock a head and listen to the unmistakable *chuff-chuff* of a nearby helicopter. "My God!" he whispered. "They must be supplied by Castro!"

As soon as everybody was aboard, Murch lifted the helicopter into the air and swung them away north into the night. They ran without lights, curving north and west over Harlem again, then dropping low over the Hudson River and heading south.

Murch was the only one who didn't know about the missing emerald, but when he saw that no one else was happy he began to understand that something must have gone wrong. He kept trying to find out what, paying no attention to the controls or the dark water rushing by just below the flimsy craft they were in, so Dortmunder finally put his cupped hands against Murch's ear and bellowed the facts into his head. Murch then wanted to turn it into a conversation, but when Dortmunder pointed at the tanker they were about to crash into in Upper Bay, Murch went back to his knitting.

They were on the ground again at the starting point at ten past eight. In the humming silence that followed Murch's shutting off of the engine no one said anything at first, until Murch commented sadly, "I'd been think-ing about buying one of these. It beats even the Belt Parkway, you know?"

Nobody answered him. They all climbed down to

the ground, all feeling stiff, and walked over to the Lincoln, now less lavender in the darkness.

There was very little talk on the drive back to Manhattan. They let Dortmunder off at his apartment and he went upstairs, made himself a bourbon on the rocks, sat down on the sofa, and looked at his briefcase full of encyclopedia brochures.

Dortmunder sighed.

PHASE
FOUR

1

"Nice doggy," Dortmunder said.

The German shepherd wasn't buying any. He stood in front of the stoop, head down, eyes up, jaws slightly open to show his pointy teeth, and said, "Rrrrrr," softly in his throat every time Dortmunder made a move to come down off the porch. The message was clear. The damn dog was going to hold him here until somebody in authority came home.

"Look, doggy," Dortmunder said, trying to be reasonable, "all I did was ring the bell. I didn't break in, I didn't steal anything, I just rang the bell. But nobody's home, so now I want to go to some other house and ring the bell."

"Rrrrrr," said the dog.

Dortmunder pointed to his attaché case. "I'm a salesman, doggy," he said. "I sell encyclopedias. Books. Big books. Doggy? Do you know from books?"

The dog didn't say anything. He just kept watching.

"All right now, dog," Dortmunder said, being very

stern. "Enough is enough. I have places to go, I don't have the time to fool around with you. I've got to make my rent money. Now, I'm leaving here and that's all there is—" He took a firm step forward.

"Rrrrrrrr!" said the dog.

Dortmunder took a quick step back. "God *damn* it, dog!" he cried. "This is ridiculous!"

The dog didn't think so. He was one of those by-the-book dogs. Rules were rules, and Dortmunder didn't rate any special favors.

Dortmunder looked around, but the neighborhood was as empty as the dog's mind. It was not quite two o'clock in the afternoon, September the seventh—three weeks and two days since the raid on the police station—and the neighborhood children were all in school. The neighborhood fathers were all at work, of course, and God alone knew where all the neighborhood mothers were. Wherever they were, Dortmunder was alone, trapped by a stupid overzealous dog on the porch of a middle-aged but comfortable home in a middle-aged but comfortable residential section of Long Island, about forty miles from Manhattan. Time was money, he had none to spare of either, and the damn dog was costing him both.

"There ought to be a law against dogs," Dortmunder said darkly. "Dogs like you in particular. You ought to be locked up somewhere."

The dog was unmoved.

"You're a menace to society," Dortmunder told him. "You're damn lucky if I don't sue you. Your owner, I mean. Sue the hell out of him."

Threats had no effect. This was clearly the kind of dog that would accept no responsibility. "I was just following orders," that would be his line.

Dortmunder looked around, but the porch was unfortunately shy of lengths of two-by-four with which to beat the dog into his master's seeded lawn. "God *damn* it!" Dortmunder said again.

Movement attracted his attention, and he looked down the block to see a brown Checker sedan with MD plates rolling slowly in his direction. Could it possibly be the owner of dog and house? If it wasn't, would it do any good for Dortmunder to holler help? He would feel foolish, calling for help in the middle of all this suburban peace and calm, but if it would do any good—

The Checker's horn honked. An arm waved from its side window. Dortmunder squinted, and there was Kelp's head, also sticking out the side window. Kelp shouted, "Hey, Dortmunder!"

"Right here!" Dortmunder shouted. He felt like a sailor stranded on a desert island for twenty years when a ship finally heaves to just offshore. He waved his attaché case over his head to attract Kelp's attention, even though Kelp obviously already knew who and where he was. "Here I am!" he shouted. "Right here!"

The Checker heaved to just offshore, and Kelp called, "Come on over here, I got news for you."

Dortmunder pointed at the dog. "Dog," he said.

Kelp frowned. The sun was in his eyes out there, so he shaded them with one hand and called, "What was that?"

"This dog here," Dortmunder called. "He won't let me off the porch."

"How come?"

"How do I know?" Dortmunder said in irritation. "Maybe I look like Sergeant Preston."

Kelp got out of the car, and on the other side Greenwood climbed out, and the two of them slowly approached. Greenwood called, "Did you try ringing the doorbell?"

"That's what started it," Dortmunder said.

The dog had become aware of the new arrivals. He backed in a quarter circle, till he could watch everybody, and remained wary.

Kelp said, "Did you do something to him?"

"All I did," Dortmunder insisted, "was ring the doorbell."

"Usually," Kelp said, "unless you actually do something to a dog, scare it or something, it—"

"Scare *it*? *Me*?"

Greenwood pointed at the dog and said, "Sit."

The dog cocked his head, puzzled.

More firmly, Greenwood said, *"Sit."*

The dog lifted out of his crouch and stood looking at Greenwood in a fair imitation of His Master's Voice. Who, he was clearly thinking, was this stranger who knew how to speak Dog?

"I told you to sit," Greenwood said, "and I mean *sit.*"

The dog could almost be seen to shrug. When in doubt, obey orders. It sat.

"Come on," Greenwood said to Dortmunder. "He won't bother you now."

"He won't?" Giving the dog mistrustful glances, Dortmunder started down off the porch.

"Don't act afraid of him," Greenwood said.

Dortmunder said, "It isn't an act," but he tried to look braver.

The dog wasn't sure. He looked at Dortmunder, at Greenwood, at Dortmunder, at Greenwood.

"Stay," said Greenwood.

Dortmunder stopped.

"Not you," Greenwood said. "The dog."

"Oh." Dortmunder came on down the rest of the stoop and walked on by the dog, who glowered at his left knee as though to be sure he'd remember it the next time they met.

"Stay," said Greenwood again, pointing at the dog, and then he turned around and followed Dortmunder and Kelp down the walk to the street and the Checker.

All three got aboard, Dortmunder in back, and Kelp drove them away from there. The dog, still sitting in the same place on the lawn, watched them carefully until they were out of sight. Possibly memorizing the license plate.

"I appreciate that," Dortmunder said. He was leaning forward with his forearms on the top of the front seat.

"Any time," Kelp said airily.

"What are you two doing out here anyway?" Dortmunder asked him. "I thought you were still working the smack."

"We're looking for you," Kelp said. "Last night you said you'd probably hit this neighborhood today, so we took a chance."

"I'm glad you did."

"Because we've got news for you. Anyway, Greenwood has."

Dortmunder turned his head to look at Greenwood. "Good news?"

"The best," Greenwood said. "Remember that emerald job?"

Dortmunder sat back as though the front seat had suddenly filled with snakes. "That again?"

Greenwood half turned in the seat to look back at him. "We can still get it," he said. "We've still got a shot at it."

"Take me back to the dog," Dortmunder said.

Kelp, looking at him in the rearview mirror, said, "Naw, listen to this. This is pretty good."

"Back to the dog," Dortmunder said. "I know when I'm well off."

"I don't blame you," Greenwood said. "I almost feel the same way. But God damn it, I've put so much effort into that stinking emerald, I hate to give up now. I had to pay out of my own pocket for a complete line of new identity papers, renounce an entire bookful of telephone numbers, give up a really good apartment at the kind of rent you can't get anymore in New York, and we still don't even have the emerald."

"That's the whole point," Dortmunder told him. "Look what's happened to you already. You really want to go back for more?"

"I want to finish the job," Greenwood said.

"It'll finish you," Dortmunder said. "I'm not usually what you'd call the superstitious type, but if ever there was a jinx job this one is it."

Kelp said, "Will you at least listen to what Greenwood has to say? Give him the courtesy and listen for a minute."

"What can he say that I don't already know?"

"Well, that's kind of the point," Kelp said. He glanced in the rearview mirror again, then back at the street. He made a left turn and said, "It seems he held out on us a little."

"I didn't hold out," Greenwood said. "Not exactly. The thing was, I was embarrassed. I got played for a sucker, and I hated to tell anybody about it until I could make up for it. You know what I mean?"

Dortmunder looked at him. "You told Prosker," he said.

Greenwood hung his head. "It seemed like a good idea at the time," he mumbled. "He was my attorney and all. And the way he explained it, if something went wrong while you guys were springing me, he could anyway get his hands on the emerald and turn it over to Iko and use the money to try to spring the whole bunch of us."

Dortmunder made a sour face. "He didn't sell you any gold mine stock, did he?"

"It seemed reasonable," Greenwood said plaintively. "Who knew he'd turn out to be a thief?"

"Everybody," Dortmunder said.

"That isn't the point," Kelp mentioned. "The point is, now we know who has the emerald."

"It's been over three weeks," Dortmunder said. "How come it took so long to deliver the news?"

Greenwood said, "I wanted to try to get the emerald back by myself. I figured you guys did enough, you went through three operations, you sprang me out of prison, I owed it to you to get the emerald back from Prosker myself."

Dortmunder gave him a cynical look.

"I swear," Greenwood said. "I wasn't going to keep it for myself, I was going to turn it over to the group."

"That's neither here nor there," Kelp said. "The point is, we know Prosker's got it. We know he didn't turn it over to Major Iko, because I checked with the Major this morning, which means he's holding on to it till the heat's off and then he'll peddle it to the highest bidder. So all we got to do is go take it away from Prosker, turn it over to Iko, and we're back in business."

"If it was that easy," Dortmunder said, "Greenwood wouldn't be here without the emerald."

"You're right," Greenwood said. "There's a little problem."

"A little problem," said Dortmunder.

"After we didn't find the emerald at the police station," Greenwood said, "naturally I went looking for Prosker."

"Naturally," said Dortmunder.

"He disappeared," Greenwood said. "He was away from the office on vacation, nobody knew when he was due back. His wife didn't know where he was, she thought he was off shacked up with somebody's secretary. That's what I've been doing the last three weeks, trying to find Prosker."

Dortmunder said, "So now you want the rest of us to help you look."

"No," said Greenwood. "I found him. Two days ago, I found out where he was. The problem is, he's going to be a little bit difficult to get at. It's going to take more than one man."

Dortmunder lowered his head and put a hand over his eyes. "You might as well go ahead and tell me," he said.

Greenwood cleared his throat. "The same day we knocked over the police station," he said, "Prosker committed himself to an insane asylum."

There was a long silence. Dortmunder didn't move. Greenwood watched him worriedly. Kelp alternately watched Dortmunder and the traffic.

Dortmunder sighed. He lowered the hand from his eyes, lifted his head. He looked very tired. He reached forward and tapped Kelp on the shoulder. "Kelp," he said.

Kelp looked in the rearview mirror. "Yeah?"

"Please take me back to the dog. Please."

2

Dortmunder's New York probation officer was an overworked and undermotivated balding man named Steen. Two days after Dortmunder was rescued from the dog by Greenwood and Kelp, he sat for one of his regular interviews in Steen's office and Steen said, "Well, it looks as though you're really going straight this time, Dortmunder. That's very good."

"I've learned my lesson," Dortmunder said.

"It's never too late to learn," Steen agreed. "But let me give you one little piece of friendly advice. In my experience, in the experience of this office and generally, the thing you've got to look out for most of all is bad companions."

Dortmunder nodded.

"Now," Steen said, "that may seem like a strange thing to say to a man your age, but the fact of the matter is, more recidivism is caused by bad companions than just about any other factor. You want to remember that, in case any of your old chums ever come to you with that just-one-more-job that's supposed to put you on Easy Street."

"I already turned 'em down," Dortmunder said heavily. "Don't you worry."

Steen looked blank. "You what?"

"I said no."

Steen shook his head. "No what?"

"No, I wouldn't do it," Dortmunder told him. He looked at Steen and saw that Steen remained unenlightened, so he told him, "The just-one-more-job guys. I told them no dice."

Steen gaped at him. "You were approached? For a robbery?"

"Sure."

"And you turned it down?"

"Damn right," Dortmunder said. "There comes a point when you got to give anything up as a bad job."

"And," said Steen, so stunned his voice was cracking, "you're reporting it to *me*?"

"Well, you brought it up," Dortmunder reminded him.

"That's right," Steen said, in a vague sort of way. "I did, didn't I?" He gazed around the bleak battered office with its grimy furniture and the faded inspirational posters on the walls, and his eyes were shining with an unaccustomed glow. He could be seen to think, It *does* work! The whole probation system, the paperwork, the irritation, the crummy offices, the surly parolees, by God it *works*! A parolee has actually been approached to take part in a crime, and has actually turned it down, and has even reported it to his probation officer! Life *does* have meaning after all!

Gradually Dortmunder began to grow impatient. He cleared his throat. He tapped his knuckles on the desk. He developed a coughing fit. Finally he said, "If you don't need me any more—"

Steen's eyes slowly refocused on him. "Dortmunder," he said, "I want you to know something. I want you to know you have made me a very happy man."

Dortmunder had no idea what the hell he was talking about. "Well, that's good," he said. "Any time I can help out."

Steen cocked his head to one side, like that dog the other day. "I don't suppose," he said, "you'd want to tell me the names of the people who contacted you?"

Dortmunder shrugged. "It was just some people," he said. He was a little sorry now he'd brought it up. Usually he wouldn't have, but this emerald business had gotten him rattled over the last few months, and the habits of a lifetime were gradually going to hell. "Just some people I used to know," he amplified, to make it clear he wasn't saying any more than that.

Steen nodded. "I understand," he said. "You still have to draw the line somewhere. Still, this has been a red-letter day for crime prevention, I want you to know that. And for me."

"That's good," Dortmunder said. He wasn't following, but it didn't matter.

Steen looked down at the paperwork on his desk. "Well, let's see. Just the usual questions left, I guess. You're still going to that machinists' school?"

"Oh, sure," Dortmunder said. There was no machinists' school, naturally.

"And you're still being supported by your cousin-in-law, is that right? Mr. Kelp."

"Sure," Dortmunder said.

"You're lucky to have such relatives," Steen said. "In fact, I wouldn't be surprised to hear that Mr. Kelp had something to do with what you told me here today."

Dortmunder frowned at him. "Oh, yeah?"

Steen, smiling happily at his paperwork again, didn't catch the expression on Dortmunder's face, which was just as well. "Well, that's about it for this time," he said and looked up, and Dortmunder's face had no expression at all.

Dortmunder got to his feet. "Be seeing you."

"Keep up the good work," Steen said. "Keep away from those bad companions."

"I'll do that," Dortmunder said and went home, and they were all sitting around his living room, drinking his booze. He shut the door and said, "Who let you birds in?"

"I did," said Chefwick. "I hope you don't mind." He was drinking ginger ale.

"Why should I mind?" Dortmunder said. "It isn't like it's a private apartment or anything."

"We wanted to talk to you," Kelp said. He was drinking Dortmunder's bourbon, and he held out a glass of the stuff, saying, "I brought out a glass for you."

Dortmunder took it and said, "I'm not breaking into any insane asylum. You people want to, you probably ought to be there anyway, so go right ahead." He turned toward his favorite chair, but Greenwood was sprawled all over it, so he sat in the uncomfortable chair with the wooden arms instead.

Kelp said, "All the rest of us are in it, Dortmunder. Everybody's willing to give it one more try except you."

Greenwood said, "We wish you'd come in with us."

"What do you need me for? Do it without me, you've got four men."

Kelp said, "You're the planner, Dortmunder, you're the organizer. We need you to run things."

Dortmunder said, "You could do it yourself. Or Greenwood. Chefwick could do it. I don't know, maybe even Murch could do it."

Murch said, "Not as good as you."

"You don't need me," Dortmunder said. "Besides, I been warned away from bad companions, and that means you bunch."

Kelp waved his hands in negation. "That horoscope stuff doesn't mean a thing," he said. "I got hooked on that stuff once, my second wife was a nut for all that. The only fall I ever took, I did what the horoscope told me."

Dortmunder frowned at him. "What the hell are you talking about?"

"Horoscope," Kelp explained. He moved his hands like a man shuffling jigsaw puzzle pieces. "Bad companions," he said. "Tall dark trips. Afternoon is good for business marriages. All that stuff."

Dortmunder squinted, trying to see Kelp clearly enough to understand him. Finally he said, in some doubt, "You mean horoscope?"

"Sure," Kelp said. "Naturally."

Dortmunder shook his head, still trying to understand. "You believe in horoscopes?"

"No," Kelp said. "You do."

Dortmunder thought about that for a few seconds, then nodded heavily and said to the room at large, "I hope you guys'll be very happy here. I'll let you know where to send my stuff." He turned and headed for the door.

Kelp said, "Hey! Wait a second!"

Chefwick came up off his chair and ran around in front of Dortmunder. "I understand how you feel," he said. "Honestly I do. At first, when Kelp and Greenwood came out to see me, I had the same attitude as you. But I listened, I let them explain it to me, and when they did—"

"That was where you made your mistake," Dortmunder told him. "Never listen to those two, they've turned all of life into a quick game of smack."

"Dortmunder," Chefwick said, "we need you. It's as simple as that. With you running things we can get this job done once and for all."

Dortmunder looked at him. "Job? Jobs, you mean. Do you realize we've already pulled three heists for that stinking emerald, and we still don't have it? And no matter how many heists we pull, our take is still the same."

Greenwood had come over now to the door, where Chefwick and Dortmunder were standing, and he said, "No, it isn't. At first it was thirty a man, and then for the police station it went up to thirty-five."

Kelp came over too, saying, "And the Major will go up again, Dortmunder, I already talked to him. Another five thousand a man. That's forty gee for walking into an insane asylum and walking back out with crazy-like-a-fox Prosker."

Dortmunder turned to him. "No, it isn't," he said. "That would be the fourth heist, and that one's a kidnapping, which is a Federal offense and they can give you the chair for it. But even just talking economics, that's the fourth heist, and four heists for forty grand is ten thousand dollars a caper, and I haven't worked a job for ten grand since I was fourteen years old."

Kelp said, "You gotta think about the living expenses too. That's another couple grand, by the time we're done. Twelve thousand dollars isn't all that bad for a heist."

"It's a jinx," Dortmunder said. "Don't give me any more horoscope stuff, all I'm saying is I'm not superstitious and I don't believe in jinxes, but there's one jinx in the world and that emerald is it."

Greenwood said, "Just look at it, Dortmunder. Just go out on the train and look at it, that's all we ask. If it doesn't look good to you, we'll forget it."

"It doesn't look good to me," Dortmunder said.

Greenwood said, "How do you *know*? You haven't even *seen* it yet."

"I don't have to," Dortmunder said. "I already know I hate it." He spread his hands. "Why don't you people just go do it yourselves? Or you need five men, get somebody else. You can even use my phone."

Chefwick said, "I think we should put our cards on the table."

Greenwood shrugged. "I suppose so," he said.

Murch, the only one still seated and still sipping

away at his beer, called, "I told you that in the first place."

Kelp said, "I just didn't want to put pressure on him like that, that's all."

Dortmunder, looking around at everybody with grim suspicion, said, "What now?"

Chefwick told him, "Iko won't finance us without you."

Greenwood said, "He's sold on you, Dortmunder, he knows you're the best man around."

"God damn it," said Dortmunder.

Kelp said, "All we want you to do is look at it. After that, if you say no go, we won't bother you any more."

"We could take the train up there tomorrow," Greenwood said.

"If you're willing," Chefwick said.

They all stood there and watched Dortmunder and waited for him to say something. He glowered at the floor and chewed his knuckle and after a while walked through them and back over to the table where he'd put down his bourbon. He picked it up, and took a healthy swallow, and turned around to look at them all.

Greenwood said, "You'll go take a look at the place?"

"I suppose so," Dortmunder said. He didn't sound happy.

Everybody else was happy. "That's great!" Kelp said.

"It'll give me a chance to get my head examined," Dortmunder said and finished his bourbon.

3

"Tickets," said the conductor.

"Air," said Dortmunder.

The conductor stood in the aisle with his punch poised. He said, "What?"

"There's no air in this car," Dortmunder told him. "The windows won't open and there isn't any air."

"You're right," the conductor said. "Could I have your tickets?"

"Could we have some air?"

"Don't ask me," said the conductor. "The railroad guarantees transportation, pick you up here, put you down there. The railroad isn't in the air business. I need your tickets."

"I need air," Dortmunder said.

"You could get off the train at the next stop," the conductor said. "Lots of air on the platform."

Kelp, sitting next to Dortmunder, tugged his sleeve and said, "Forget it. You're not gonna get anywhere."

Dortmunder looked at the conductor's face and saw

that Kelp was right. He shrugged and handed over his ticket, and Kelp did the same, and the conductor made holes in them before giving them back. Then he did the same for Murch, across the aisle, and for Greenwood and Chefwick in the next seat back. Since the five were the only occupants of this car, the conductor then strolled slowly down the aisle and out the far end, leaving them once again alone.

Kelp said, "You never get any satisfaction from those union types."

"Sure," said Dortmunder. He looked around and said, "Anybody carrying?"

Kelp looked startled, saying, "Dortmunder! You don't bump off a guy for no air!"

"Who said anything about bump off? Isn't anybody heavy?"

"Me," said Greenwood, and from inside his Norfolk jacket—he was the spiffiest dresser in the group—he produced a Smith and Wesson Terrier, a five-shot .32 caliber revolver with a two-inch barrel. He handed it over to Dortmunder, butt first, and Dortmunder said, "Thanks." He took the gun, reversed it to hold it by the barrel and chamber, and said to Kelp, "Excuse me." Then he leaned across Kelp and punched a hole in the window.

"Hey!" said Kelp.

"Air," said Dortmunder. He turned and handed the gun back to Greenwood, saying, "Thanks again."

Greenwood looked a little dazed. "Any time," he said and looked at the butt, studying it for scratches. There weren't any, and he put it away again.

This was Sunday, the tenth of September, and they were on just about the only passenger train running in this direction on Sunday. The occasional platform they stopped beside was empty except for those three old men in baggy work pants who lean against the wall of every small-town railroad station platform in the United States. The sun was shining outside, and the fresh air blowing in through the hole Dortmunder had made was pleasantly scented with the odors of late summer. The train clackety-clacked along at a contemplative seventeen miles an hour, giving the passengers an opportunity to really study the landscape, and all in all it was the pleasant sort of leisurely excursion you just can't find too often in the twentieth century.

"How much longer?" Dortmunder said.

Kelp looked at his watch. "Another ten or fifteen minutes," he said. "You'll be able to see the place from the train. On this side."

Dortmunder nodded.

"It's a big old brick place," Kelp said. "It used to be a factory, they used to make prefabricated fallout shelters there."

Dortmunder looked at him. "Every time you start to talk to me," he said, "you tell me more facts than I want to know. Prefabricated fallout shelters. I don't want to know why the factory went bust."

"It's a pretty interesting story," Kelp said.

"I figured it probably was."

The train stopped just then and Dortmunder and Kelp looked out at the three old men, who looked back. The train started up again, and Kelp said, "We're the next stop."

"What's the name of the town?"

"New Mycenae. It's named after an old Greek city."

"I don't want to know why," Dortmunder said.

Kelp turned to look at him. "What's the matter with you?"

"Nothing," said Dortmunder, and the conductor came back into the car and walked down the aisle and stopped beside them. He frowned at the hole in the window. He said, "Who did that?"

"An old man back at that last station," Dortmunder said.

The conductor glared at him. "You did it," he said.

Kelp said, "No, he didn't. An old man did, back at that last station."

Greenwood, in the next seat back, said, "That's right. I saw it happen. An old man did it, back at the last station."

The conductor glowered around at everybody. "You expect me to believe that?"

Nobody answered him.

He frowned some more at the hole in the window, then turned around to Murch, sitting across the aisle. "Did you see it?"

"Sure," Murch said.

"What happened?"

"An old man did it," Murch said. "Back at that last station."

The conductor lowered an eyebrow at him. "You with these people?"

"Never saw them before in my life," Murch said.

The conductor gave everybody suspicious looks, then mumbled something nobody could make out and turned away and walked down to the end of the car. He went out the door, and popped back in a second later to call, "Next stop New McKinney," as though daring somebody to make something of it. He glared, waited, then disappeared again and slammed the door.

Dortmunder said to Kelp, "I thought you said the next stop was us."

"It's supposed to be," said Kelp. He looked out the window and said, "Sure it is. There's the place."

Dortmunder looked where Kelp was pointing and saw a large sprawling red brick building off to the right a ways. A tall chain-link fence enclosed the grounds, with metal signs attached to it at intervals. Dortmunder squinted, but couldn't make out what the signs said. He said to Kelp, "What do the signs say?"

"Danger," Kelp told him. "High voltage."

Dortmunder looked at him, but Kelp was gazing out the window, refusing to meet his eye. Dortmunder shook his head and looked out at the asylum again, seeing a set of tracks that curved away from the tracks the train was on and angled around to go under the electrified fence and across the asylum grounds. The tracks were orange with rust, and within the grounds they'd been incorporated in the design of a formal flower bed. A couple of dozen people in white pajamas and white bathrobes were strolling around the grass in there, being watched by what looked like armed guards in blue uniforms.

"So far," Dortmunder said, "I wouldn't say it looks easy."

"Give it a chance," Kelp said.

The train had started to slow, as the asylum moved into the background, and now the door at the far end of the car opened again and the conductor stuck his head in to call, "New McKinney! *Newwww* McKinney!"

Kelp and Dortmunder frowned at each other. They looked out the window, and the platform was just edging into sight. The sign on it said, NEW MYCENAE.

"New McKinney!" yelled the conductor.

"I think I hate him," Dortmunder said. He got to his feet, and the other four got up after him. They went down the aisle as the train creaked to a stop, and the conductor glowered at them as they disembarked. He said to Murch, "I thought you said you weren't with these guys."

"With who?" Murch asked him and went on down to the platform.

The train started up and stumbled slowly away from the station, the conductor leaning out for a long while to look after his five passengers. The three old men on the platform studied them too, one of them spitting tobacco juice to mark the occasion.

Dortmunder and the others walked through the station and out the other side, where they turned down a mustached fat man who claimed his 1949 Fraser was a cab.

"We can walk it," Kelp told Dortmunder. "It isn't far."

It wasn't. They walked about seven blocks and then

they came to the main entrance, with a sign to one side reading, "Clair de Lune Sanitarium." The electrified fence was set back from the road here, with another chain-link fence about five feet in front of it. Two armed guards sat on folding chairs inside the main gate, chatting together.

Dortmunder stopped and looked at it all. "Who've they got in there?" he said. "Rudolf Hess?"

"It's what they call a maximum security bughouse," Kelp told him. "For rich nuts only. Most of them in there are what they call criminally insane, but their family has enough money to keep them out of some state asylum."

"I've wasted a whole day," Dortmunder said. "I could of sold half a dozen encyclopedias today. Sunday's a good day for encyclopedias, you got the husband at home, you tell the husband you'll throw in a bookcase that comes unassembled and he can put it together himself, and he'll hand you his wallet."

Chefwick said, "You mean it can't be done?"

"Armed guards," Dortmunder said. "Electrified fences. Not to speak of the inmates. You want to mix with *them*?"

Greenwood said, "I was hoping you'd see some way. There oughta be a way to get in there."

"Sure there's a way to get in there," Dortmunder said. "You drop in with a parachute. Now let's see you get *out*."

Murch said, "Why don't we walk around the place? Maybe we'll see something."

"Like antiaircraft guns," Dortmunder said. "That is not an easy nuthouse to crack."

Kelp said, "We got an hour to kill before our train back. We might as well walk around."

Dortmunder shrugged. "All right, we'll walk around."

They walked around, and they didn't see anything encouraging. When they got to the rear of the building, they had to leave blacktopped road and walk across scrubby field. They stepped over the rusty orange tracks, and Chefwick said primly, "I keep *my* tracks in better condition than this."

"Well, they don't use these any more," Kelp said.

Murch said, "Look, one of the loonies is waving at us."

They looked, and it was true. One of the figures in white stood by the flower bed and waved at them. He was shielding his eyes from the sun with his other hand, and he was smiling to beat the band.

They started to wave back to him, and then Greenwood said, "Hey! That's Prosker!"

Everybody stood there with his hand up in the air. Chefwick said, "So it is." He pulled his hand down, and everybody else followed suit. In there by the flower bed Prosker waved and waved, and then began to laugh. He bent over and slapped his knee and went into a fit of laughter. He tried to wave and laugh at the same time and almost fell over.

Dortmunder said, "Greenwood, let me borrow it again."

"No, Dortmunder," said Kelp. "We need him to give us the emerald."

"Except we can't get at him," Murch said. "So it doesn't make any difference."

"We'll see about that," said Dortmunder, and shook his fist at Prosker, who as a result laughed so hard he sat down on the ground. A guard came over and looked at him, but didn't do anything.

Kelp said, "I hate it that we're beaten by a louse like that."

"We aren't," Dortmunder said grimly.

They all looked at him. Kelp said, "You mean—?"

"He can't laugh at me," Dortmunder said. "I've had enough, that's all."

"You mean we're going in after him?"

"I mean I've had enough," Dortmunder said. He looked at Kelp. "You go tell Iko to put us back on the payroll," he said and looked back at Prosker, who was now rolling around on the ground, clutching his ribcage and beating his heels into the turf. "If he thinks he can stay in that place," Dortmunder said, "he's crazy."

4

When the ebony man showed Kelp in, Major Iko was leaning over the pool table sighting down the cue like a sniper with a musket. Kelp looked at the lie of the table and said, "You go for the twelve like that, your cue ball is going to ricochet off the three and drop the eight."

Without moving, the Major lifted his eyes and looked at Kelp. "You're wrong," he said. "I have been practicing."

Kelp shrugged. "Go ahead," he said.

The Major sighted some more, then hit the cue ball, which hit the twelve, ricocheted off the three, and dropped the eight. *"Banimi ka junt!"* the Major said and threw the cue down onto the table. "Well?" he barked at Kelp. "It's been two weeks since Dortmunder agreed to do the job. Money keeps going out, but no emerald ever comes in."

"We're ready again," Kelp said and pulled a tattered list from his pocket. "This is the stuff we need."

"No helicopters this time, I hope."

"No, it's too far from New York. But we thought about it."

"I'm sure you did," the Major said dryly and took the list.

Kelp said, "Mind if I sink a couple?"

"Go ahead," the Major said and opened the sheet of paper.

Kelp picked up the cue, dropped the three, and the Major screamed, "A *locomotive*?"

Kelp nodded and put the cue down again. Turning to face the Major, he said, "Dortmunder thought there might be some question about that."

"Question!" The Major looked as though he'd been poleaxed.

"We don't actually need a big diesel locomotive," Kelp said. "What we need is something that runs on standard gauge tracks under its own power. But it's got to be bigger than a handcar."

"Bigger than a handcar," the Major said. He backed up till his legs hit a chair, on which he sat. The list hung forgotten in his hand.

"Chefwick is our railroad expert," Kelp said. "So if you want to talk things over with him, he'll let you know exactly what we need."

"Of course," the Major said.

"He could come over tomorrow afternoon," Kelp suggested.

"Of course," the Major said.

"If you could have your own people ready by then. For him to talk to."

"Of course," the Major said.

Kelp frowned at him. "You okay, Major?"

"Of course," the Major said.

Kelp went over and waved his hand in front of the Major's eyes. They didn't change, they kept staring at some point in the middle of the room. Kelp said, "Maybe I oughta give you a call later on. When you're feeling better."

"Of course," the Major said.

"It really isn't that big a locomotive we want," Kelp said. "Just a kind of a medium-size locomotive."

"Of course," the Major said.

"Well." Kelp looked around a little helplessly. "I'll call you later on," he said. "About when Chefwick should come over."

"Of course," the Major said.

Kelp backed to the doorway and hesitated there for a second, feeling the need to say something to buck the Major's spirits up a little. "Your pool is getting a lot better, Major," he said at last.

"Of course," the Major said.

5

Major Iko stood beside the truck, forehead furrowed with worry. "I've got to give this locomotive back," he said. "Don't lose it, don't hurt it. I have to give it back, it's only borrowed."

"You'll get it back," Dortmunder assured him. He checked his watch and said, "We've got to get going."

"Be careful with the locomotive," the Major pleaded. "That's all I ask."

Chefwick said, "You have my personal word of honor, Major, that no harm will come to this locomotive. I think you know my feeling about locomotives."

The Major nodded, somewhat reassured, but still worried. A muscle in his cheek was jumping.

"Time to go," Dortmunder said. "See you later, Major."

Murch would drive, of course, and Dortmunder sat in the cab beside him, while the other three got in back with the locomotive. The Major stood watching them, and Murch waved to him and drove the truck down the dirt road from the deserted farmhouse and out to the highway, where he turned north, away from New York and toward New Mycenae.

It was a very anonymous truck, with an ordinary red cab and a trailer completely swathed in olive drab tarpaulins, and no one they passed gave them a second look. But underneath the tarps lurked a very gaudy truck indeed, its sides combining brightly painted pictures of railroading scenes with foot-high red letters running the length of the trailer and reading, FUN ISLAND AMUSEMENT PARK—TOM THUMB. And underneath, in slightly smaller black lettering, THE FAMOUS LOCOMOTIVE.

What strings the Major had pulled, what stories he'd told, what bribes he'd paid, what pressures he'd applied in order to get this locomotive, Dortmunder neither knew nor cared. He'd gotten it, that was all, within two weeks of the order having been placed, and now Dortmunder was going to go wipe that laugh from Attorney Prosker's face. Oh, yes, he would.

This was the second Sunday in October, sunny but cool, with little traffic on the secondary roads they were traveling, and they made good time to New Mycenae. Murch drove them through town and out the road toward the Clair de Lune Sanitarium. They rode on by, and Dortmunder glanced at it as they went past. Peaceful. Same two guards chatting at the main gate. Everything the same.

They traveled another three miles down the same road, and then Murch turned right. Half a mile later he pulled off to the side of the road and stopped, pulling on the handbrake but leaving the engine running. This was a woodsy, hilly area, without houses or other buildings. A hundred yards ahead stood a set of white crossbars, warning of a railroad crossing.

Dortmunder looked at his watch. "Due in four minutes," he said.

In the last two weeks, he and the others had been all over this territory, till they knew it now as well as they knew their own homes. They knew which roads were well traveled and which were generally empty. They knew where a lot of the dirt side roads went, they knew what the local police cars looked like and where they tended to spend their Sunday afternoons, they knew four or five good places in the neighborhood to hide out with a truck, and they knew the railroad schedule.

Better than the railroad did, evidently, because the train Dortmunder was waiting for was almost five minutes late. But at last they did hear it hooting in the distance, and then slowly it appeared and began to trundle by, the same passenger train Dortmunder and the others had ridden up here in two weeks ago.

"There's your window," Murch said and pointed at a holed window gliding by.

"I didn't think they'd fix it," Dortmunder said.

It takes a train quite a while to get itself entirely past a given point, particularly at seventeen miles an hour, but eventually the final car did go by and the road was once again clear. Murch looked at Dortmunder and said, "How long?"

"Give it a couple minutes."

They knew the next scheduled occupant of that track

would be a southbound freight at nine-thirty tonight. During the week there were many trains going back and forth, both passenger and freight, but on Sundays most trains stayed home.

After a minute or two of silence, Dortmunder dropped his Camel butt on the truck floor and stepped on it. "We can go now," he said.

"Right." Murch put the truck in gear and eased forward to the tracks. He jockeyed back and forth till he was crosswise on the road, blocking it, and then Dortmunder got out and went around back to open the rear doors. Greenwood and Kelp at once began to push forward a long complicated boardlike object, a wide metal ramp with a set of railroad tracks on it. The far end clanged on the rails below, and Greenwood came down to help Dortmunder push and shove it till the ramp's tracks lined up with the railroad company's tracks. Then Greenwood waved to Kelp on the tailgate, who turned around and waved into the interior, and a few seconds later a locomotive came out.

And what a locomotive. This was Tom Thumb, the *famous* locomotive, or at any rate a replica of the famous Tom Thumb, the original of which, built for the Baltimore & Ohio back in 1830, was the first regularly working American-built steam locomotive. It looked just like all the old, old locomotives in Walt Disney movies and so did the replica, which was an exact copy of the original. Well, maybe not exactly exact, since there were one or two small differences, such as that the original Tom Thumb ran on steam from a coal-fired furnace while the replica ran on gasoline in an engine from a 1962

Ford. But it looked legit, that was the important thing, and who was going to carp about the thin putt-putt of smoke that snuck out the tailgate instead of the thick belch-belch of smoke that was supposed to issue from the funnel-mouth smokestack?

Apparently this replica didn't spend all its time in the amusement park mentioned on its mother truck, but at least occasionally traveled around to be displayed at fairs and supermarket openings and other gala events. The specially equipped truck was itself an indication of that, as was the fact that the wheels were suited to the standard gauge of today's tracks.

The locomotive came complete with its own tender, a boxlike wooden affair like a dinette on wheels. On the original the tender was usually full of coal, but in the replica it was empty except for a green-handled push-broom leaning against one corner.

Chefwick was at the controls as Tom Thumb came slowly down the ramp and effected the tricky transition from one set of rails to another, and he was in seventh heaven, smiling and beaming around in sheer delight. In his mind he hadn't been given a full-size locomotive, he himself had been miniaturized. He was running a model train *in person*. He beamed out at Dortmunder and said, "Toot toot."

"Sure thing," Dortmunder said. "Up a little more."

Chefwick eased Tom Thumb forward a few more feet.

"That's good right there," Dortmunder said and went back to help Greenwood and Kelp slide the ramp back up into the truck. They shut the truck doors and hollered to Murch, who hollered back and drove the truck around in a wide loop that left it once more off the road. So far, there'd been no other traffic at all.

Chefwick and Greenwood and Kelp were already in their wet-suits, the black rubber gleaming and glistening in the sun. They weren't wearing the gloves or face masks or headpieces yet, but otherwise they were completely encased in rubber. So much for electrified fences.

Dortmunder and Greenwood and Kelp all climbed aboard the tender, and Dortmunder called forward to Chefwick, "Go ahead."

"Right," said Chefwick. "Toot toot," he called, and Tom Thumb began to perk along the track.

The other wet suit was waiting for Dortmunder in the tender, on the arms case. He put it on and said, "Remember. When we go through keep your hands over your faces."

"Right," said Kelp.

Tom Thumb traveled faster than seventeen miles an hour, and they reached the Clair de Lune Sanitarium in no time, where Chefwick pulled to a stop just before the turnoff where the old tracks angled away toward the sanitarium grounds. Greenwood jumped down, went over to the switch beside the tracks and turned it to the spur position, and then climbed back aboard.

(It had taken two nights of oiling and straining and heaving to get the old switch to work again. It's too expensive for railroads to remove all their old unused equipment, and it doesn't hurt anything to leave it all lying there, which is why there are so many abandoned stretches of track to be seen around the United States.

But there's nothing wrong with most of it except rust, which had been the only problem here. The switch now turned like a dream.)

They all put on their headpieces and gloves and face masks, and Chefwick accelerated over the bumpy orange track toward the sanitarium fencing. Tom Thumb, tender and all, was still lighter than the Ford from which his engine had come, and he accelerated like a go-cart, hitting sixty before he hit the fence.

Snap! Sparks, sputters, smoke. Live wires whipping back and forth. Tom Thumb's wheels shrieking and squealing along the twisty old rails, then shrieking even louder when Chefwick applied the brakes. They'd breached the fence like a sprinter breasting the tape, and now they screamed and scraped to a stop surrounded by chrysanthemums and gardenias.

In his office on the opposite side of the building, Chief Administrator Doctor Panchard L. Whiskum sat at his desk rereading the piece he'd just written for the *American Journal of Applied Pan-Psychotherapy*, entitled "Instances of Induced Hallucination among Staff Members of Mental Hospitals," when a white-jacketed male nurse ran in shouting, "Doctor! There's a locomotive in the garden!"

Doctor Whiskum looked at the male nurse. He looked at his manuscript. He looked at the male nurse. He looked at his manuscript. He looked at the male nurse. He said, "Sit down, Foster. Let's talk about it."

In the garden, Dortmunder and Greenwood and Kelp had emerged from the tender in wet-suits and skin divers' masks, carrying tommy guns. All over the lawn, white-garbed patients and blue-garbed guards and white-garbed attendants were running back and forth, up and down, around in circles, shouting at each other, grabbing each other, bumping into each other. Bedlam was in bedlam.

Dortmunder pointed his tommy gun in the air and let go with a burst, and the silence after that was like the silence in a cafeteria just after somebody has dropped a thousand metal trays on a tile floor. Silent. Very silent.

The lawn was full of eyes, all of them round. Dortmunder looked among them and finally found Prosker's. He pointed the tommy gun at Prosker and called, "Prosker! Get over here!"

Prosker tried to make believe he was somebody else, named Doe or Roe. He kept on standing there, pretending Dortmunder wasn't looking at him.

Dortmunder called, "Do I shoot your ankles off and have somebody carry you? Get over here."

A lady doctor in the foreground, wearing black horn-rims and white lab coat, suddenly cried, "You people ought to be ashamed of yourselves! Do you realize what you're doing to the reality concepts we're trying to instill in these people? How do you expect them to differentiate between illusion and reality when you do something like *this*?"

"Be quiet," Dortmunder told her and called to Prosker, "I'm losing my patience."

But Prosker continued to stand there, feigning innocence, until all at once a guard near him took a quick step and shoved him, shouting, "Will you get over there? Who knows if his aim is any good? You want to kill innocent people?"

A chorus of yeahs followed that remark, and the tableau of people—Living Chessboard is what it mostly looked like—turned itself into a sort of bucket brigade, pushing Prosker on from hand to hand all across the lawn to the locomotive.

When he got there, Prosker suddenly became voluble. "I'm not a well man!" he cried. "I've had illnesses, troubles, my memory's gone! I wouldn't be here, why would I be here if I wasn't a sick man. I tell you, my memory's gone, I don't know anything about anything."

"Just get up here," Dortmunder said. "We'll remind you."

Very reluctantly, with much pushing from behind and pulling from in front, Prosker got up into the tender. Kelp and Greenwood held him while Dortmunder told the crowd to stay where it was while they made their escape. "Also," he said, "send somebody to put that switch back after we're gone. We don't want to derail any trains, do we?"

A hundred heads shook no.

"Right," Dortmunder said. He told Chefwick, "Back her up."

"A-okay," Chefwick said, and under his breath he said, "Toot toot." He didn't want to say it aloud with a lot of crazy people within earshot, they might get the wrong idea.

The locomotive backed slowly out of the flower beds. Dortmunder and Kelp and Greenwood surrounded Prosker, grabbing him by the elbows and lifting him a few inches into the air. He hung there, pressed in by wet-suits on all sides, his slippered feet waggling inches above the floor, and said, "What are you doing? Why are you doing this?"

"So you don't get electrocuted," Greenwood told him. "We're about to back through live wires. Cooperate, Mr. Prosker."

"Oh, I'll cooperate," Prosker said. "I'll cooperate."

"Yes, you will," Dortmunder said.

6

Murch stood beside the tracks, smoking a Marlboro and thinking about railroad trains. What would it be like to drive a railroad train, a real one, a modern diesel? Of course, you couldn't change lanes when you wanted, but it nevertheless might be interesting, very interesting.

In the last fifteen minutes one vehicle had gone by, westbound, an ancient green pickup truck with an ancient gray farmer at the wheel. A lot of metal things in the back had gone *klank* when the truck had crossed the tracks, and the farmer had given Murch a dirty look, as though he suspected Murch of being responsible for the noise.

The other noise had come a minute or two later, being a brief stutter of tommy-gun fire, faint and far-away. Murch had listened carefully, but it hadn't been repeated. Probably just a warning, not an indication of trouble.

And now, here came something down the tracks.

Murch leaned forward, peering, and it was good old Tom Thumb, backing down the rails, its Ford engine whining in reverse.

Good. Murch flipped away the Marlboro and ran over to the truck. He backed it around into position, and had it all ready when Tom Thumb arrived.

Chefwick eased the locomotive to a stop a few yards from the rear of the truck. He was already looking a little sad at the prospect of being returned to normal size, but there was no alternative. His Drink-Me was all used up.

While Greenwood stood guard over Prosker in the tender, Dortmunder and Kelp, no longer in their wet-suits, got out and lowered the ramp into place. Chefwick backed the locomotive carefully up into the truck, and then Dortmunder and Kelp shoved the ramp back inside. Kelp climbed into the truck, and Dortmunder shut the door and went around to get into the cab with Murch.

Murch said, "Everything okay?"

"No problems."

"Nearest place?"

"Might as well," Dortmunder said.

Murch put the truck in gear and started off, and two miles later he made a sweeping left onto a narrow dirt road, one of the many dirt roads they'd checked out in the last two weeks. This one, they knew, trailed off into the woods without ever getting much of anywhere. There were small indications in the first half mile or so that it was sometimes used as a lovers' lane, but farther along the ruts grew narrower and grassier and finally petered out entirely in the middle of a dry valley, with no signs of man except a couple of meandering lines of stones that had once been boundary fences and were now mostly crumbled away. Perhaps there had once been a farm here, or even a whole town. The wooded lands of the north-eastern states are full of long-ago-abandoned farms and abandoned rural towns, some of them gone now without a trace, some still indicated by an occasional bit of stone wall or a half-buried tombstone to mark where the churchyard used to be.

Murch drove the truck in as far as he dared and stopped. "Listen to the silence," he said.

It was late afternoon now, and the woods were without sound. It was a softer, more muffled silence than the one at the sanitarium following Dortmunder's tommy-gun burst, but just as complete.

Dortmunder got out of the cab, and when he slammed the door it echoed like war noises through the trees. Murch had gotten out on the other side, and they walked separately along the trailer, meeting again at the far end. All around them stood the tree trunks, and underfoot orange and red dead leaves. Leaves still covered the branches too and fluttered constantly downward, making steady small movements down through the air that kept Dortmunder making quick sharp glances to left and right.

Dortmunder opened the rear door and he and Murch climbed inside, then shut the door again after themselves. The interior of the trailer was lit by three frosted-glass lights spaced along the top, and the place was very, very full of locomotive, with no room at all to move on the right side and just barely enough to sidle along on the left. Dortmunder and Murch went along to the front of the tender and stepped aboard.

Prosker was sitting on the arms case, his innocent-amnesiac expression beginning to fray at the edges. Kelp and Greenwood and Chefwick were standing around looking at him. There were no guns in sight.

Dortmunder went over to him and said, "Prosker, it's as simple as can be. If we're out the emerald, you're out of life. Cough it up."

Prosker looked up at Dortmunder, as innocent as a puppy who's missed the paper, and said, "I don't know what anybody's talking about. I'm a sick man."

Greenwood, in disgust, said, "Let's tie him to the tracks and run the train over him a few times. Maybe he'll talk then."

"I really doubt it," Chefwick said.

Dortmunder said, "Murch, Kelp, take him back and show him where we are."

"Right." Murch and Kelp took Prosker ungently by the elbows, hustled him off the tender, and shoved him down the narrow aisle to the rear of the truck. They pushed open a door and showed him the woods, with the late afternoon sunlight making diagonal rays down through the foliage, and when he'd seen it they shut the door again and brought him back and sat him down once more on the arms case.

Dortmunder said, "We're in the woods. Am I right?"

"Yes," Prosker said and nodded. "We're in the woods."

"You remember about woods. That's good. Look up

there in the driver's part of the locomotive. What's that leaning against the side there?"

"A shovel," Prosker said.

"You remember shovels too," Dortmunder said. "I'm glad to hear that. Do you remember about graves?"

Prosker's innocent look crumpled a little more. "You wouldn't do that to a sick man," he said and put one hand feebly to his heart.

"No," Dortmunder said. "But I'd do it to a dead man." He let Prosker think about that for a few seconds and then said, "I'll tell you what's going to happen. We're going to stay here tonight, let the cops travel around looking for a locomotive someplace. Tomorrow morning we're going to leave. If you've handed over the emerald by then, we'll let you go and you can tell the law you escaped and you didn't know what it was all about. You won't mention any names, naturally, or we'll come get you out again. You know now we can get you wherever you hide, don't you?"

Prosker looked around at the locomotive and the tender and the hard faces. "Oh, yes," he said. "Yes, I know that."

"Good," Dortmunder said. "How are you with a shovel?"

Prosker looked startled. "A shovel?"

"In case you don't give us the emerald," Dortmunder explained. "We'll be leaving here without you in the morning, and we won't want anybody finding you, so you'll have to dig a hole."

Prosker licked his lips. "I," he said. He looked at all the faces again. "I wish I could help you," he said. "I really do. But I'm a sick man. I had business reverses, personal problems, an unfaithful mistress, trouble with the Bar Association, I had a breakdown. Why do you think I was in the sanitarium?"

"Hiding from us," Dortmunder said. "You committed yourself. If you could remember enough to commit yourself to a maximum security insane asylum, you can remember enough to turn over the emerald."

"I don't know what to say," Prosker said.

"That's all right," Dortmunder told him. "You've got all night to think it over."

7

Is this deep enough?"

Dortmunder came over and looked at the hole. Prosker was standing in it in his white pajamas, his bathrobe over beside a tree. The hole was knee-deep now, and Prosker was sweating even though the morning air was cool. It was another sunny day, with the crisp clean air of the woods in autumn, but Prosker looked like August and no air conditioner.

"That's shallow," Dortmunder told him. "You want a shallow grave? That's for mugs and college girls. Don't you have any self-respect?"

"You wouldn't really kill me," Prosker said, panting. "Not for mere money. A human life is more important than money, you have to have more humanity than—"

Greenwood came over and said, "Prosker, *I'd* kill you just out of general irritation. You conned me, Prosker, *you* conned *me*. You gave everybody a lot of trouble, and I'm to blame, and in a way I hope you keep pulling the lost memory bit right up till it's time to leave."

Prosker looked pained and glanced along the trail the truck had come on. Dortmunder saw that and said, "Forget it, Prosker. If you're stalling, waiting for a lot of motorcycle cops to come racing through the trees, just give it up. It isn't gonna happen. We picked this place because it's safe."

Prosker studied Dortmunder's face, and his own face had finally lost its pained-innocence expression, replaced by a look of calculation. He thought things over for a while and then flung the shovel down and briskly said, "All right. You people wouldn't kill me, you aren't murderers, but I can see you aren't going to give up. And it looks like I won't get rescued. Help me up out of here, and we'll talk." His whole manner had abruptly changed, his voice deeper and more assured, his body straighter, his gestures quick and firm.

Dortmunder and Greenwood gave him a hand out of the hole, and Greenwood said, "Don't be so sure about *me,* Prosker."

Prosker looked at him. "You're a ladykiller, my boy," he said. "Not exactly the same thing."

"Well, you're no lady," Greenwood told him.

Dortmunder said, "The emerald."

Prosker turned to him. "Let me ask you a hypothetical question. Would you let me out of your sight before I handed over the emerald?"

"That isn't even funny," Dortmunder said.

"That's what I thought," Prosker said, and spread his hands, saying, "In that case, I'm sorry, but you'll never get it."

"I *am* gonna kill him!" Greenwood shouted, and

Murch and Chefwick and Kelp strolled over to listen to the conversation.

"Explain," Dortmunder said.

Prosker said, "The emerald is in my safe deposit box in a bank on Fifth Avenue and Forty-sixth Street in Manhattan. It takes two keys to open the box, mine and the bank's. The bank regulations require that I go down into the vault accompanied only by an officer of the bank. The two of us have to be alone, and in the vault I have to sign their book, and they compare the signature with the specimen they keep on file. In other words, it has to be me and I have to be alone. If I gave you my word I wouldn't tell the bank officer to call the police while we were down there you wouldn't trust me, and I wouldn't blame you. I wouldn't believe it myself. You can mount a perpetual watch on the bank if you wish, and kidnap and search me every time I go into it and come out, but that only means the emerald will stay where it is, useless to me and useless to you."

"God damn it," said Dortmunder.

"I'm sorry," Prosker said. "I'm truly sorry. If I'd left the stone anywhere else, I'm sure we could have worked out some arrangement where I would be reimbursed for my time and expenses—"

"I ought to rap you in the mouth!" Greenwood shouted.

"Be quiet," Dortmunder told him. To Prosker he said, "Go on."

Prosker shrugged. "The problem is insoluble," he said. "I put the stone where neither of us can get it."

Dortmunder said, "Where's your key?"

"To the box? In my office in town. Hidden. If you're thinking of sending someone in my place to forge my signature, let me be a good sport and warn you that two of the bank's officers know me fairly well. It's possible your forger wouldn't meet either of those two, but I don't think you should count on it."

Greenwood said, "Dortmunder, what if this louse was to die? His wife would inherit, right? Then we'd get the stone from *her*."

Prosker said, "No, that wouldn't work either. In the event of my death, the box would be opened in the presence of my wife, two bank officers, my wife's attorney and no doubt someone from Probate Court. I'm afraid my wife would never get to take the emerald home with her."

"God damn it to *hell*," said Dortmunder.

Kelp said, "You know what this means, Dortmunder."

"I don't want to hear about it," Dortmunder said.

"We get to rob a bank," Kelp said.

"Just don't talk to me," Dortmunder said.

"I am sorry," Prosker said briskly. "But there's nothing to be done," he said, and Greenwood hit him in the eye, and he fell backwards into the hole.

"Where's the shovel?" Greenwood said, but Dortmunder said, "Forget that. Get him up out of there, and back in the truck."

Murch said, "Where we going?"

"Back to the city," Dortmunder said. "To make the Major's day."

PHASE
FIVE

PHASE
FIVE

1

"I am not happy," the Major said.

"On the other hand," Dortmunder said, "I'm giggling all over."

They were all sitting around the Major's office, having arrived in time to interrupt his lunch. Prosker, in dirt-stained pajamas and bathrobe, was sitting in the middle, where everyone could see him. The Major was behind his desk, and Dortmunder and the others were grouped in a semicircle facing him.

Prosker said, "I continue to be sincerely sorry. It was shortsighted of me, but I moved in haste and now regret in leisure." He had a nicely developing black eye.

"Just shut up," Greenwood told him, "or I'll give you something else to regret."

"I hired you people in the first place," the Major said, "because you were supposed to be professionals, you were supposed to know how to do the job right."

Kelp, stung, said, "We are professionals, Major, and we did do the job right. We've done four jobs, and we did them *all* right. We got away with the emerald. We broke Greenwood out of jail. We got into the police station and back out again. And we kidnaped Prosker from the asylum. We've done everything right."

"Then why," the Major said angrily, "don't I have the Balabomo Emerald?" He held a hand out, empty palm up, to demonstrate that he didn't have it.

"Circumstances," Kelp said. "Circumstances have conspired against us."

The Major snorted.

Chefwick said, "Major, at the moment you are short-tempered, and it's perfectly understandable. But so are we, and also with justification. I won't speak for myself, Major, but I will tell you that in my twenty-three years in this business I have gotten to know a large number of people engaged in it, and I assure you this team could not be improved upon anywhere."

"That's right," Kelp said. "Take Dortmunder. That man's a genius. He's sat down and worked out four capers in four months and brought every last one of them off. There isn't another man in the business could have done that. There isn't another man in the business could have organized the Prosker kidnaping *alone,* much less the other three jobs."

Greenwood said, "And what Chefwick said about the rest of us goes double for Chefwick, because not only is he one of the best lockmen in the business, he is a grade-A first-class railroad engineer."

Chefwick blushed with pleasure and embarrassment.

The Major said, "Before you all start proposing toasts

to one another, let me remind you that *I still do not have the Balabomo Emerald.*"

"We know that, Major," said Dortmunder. "We still don't have our forty grand each either."

"You're getting it an inch at a time," the Major said angrily. "Do you realize I have so far paid out over twelve thousand dollars to you people in salaries alone? Plus nearly eight thousand in material and supplies for all these practice robberies you keep performing. Twenty thousand dollars, and what do I have to show for it? The operation was successful, but the patient died. It just won't do. It won't do any more, and that's final."

Dortmunder heaved himself to his feet. "That's all right by me, Major," he said. "I came down here willing to give it one more try, but if you want to call it off I won't fight you. Tomorrow's an anniversary for me, I'll be out of the pen four months tomorrow, and all I've done in all that time is run around after that goddamn emerald of yours. I'm sick of it, if you want the truth, and if Prosker hadn't goaded me into it I would have quit before this caper."

"Something else for me to be sorry for," Prosker said fatalistically.

"Shut up, you," Greenwood said.

Kelp was on his feet, saying, "Dortmunder, don't get mad. You too, Major, there's no point everybody getting mad at everybody. This time we know for sure where the emerald is."

"If Prosker isn't lying," the Major said.

"Not me, Major," Prosker said.

"I said shut up," Greenwood said.

"He isn't lying," Kelp said. "He knows if we get into that bank and there's no emerald, we'll come back to see him and this time we'll get rough."

"A smart lawyer knows when to tell the truth," Prosker said.

Greenwood leaned over and rapped Prosker on the knee. "You didn't shut up yet," he said.

Kelp was saying, "The point is, this time we know for sure where it is. It's there, and it can't be moved. We've got the only guy who could move it, and we're holding on to him. If we just do our jobs like we always do, the stone is ours. So we don't have to get mad at each other. It isn't your fault, Major, and it isn't your fault, Dortmunder, it's just the breaks of the game. One more caper and we're done, it's over, and everybody's still friends."

"I've heard of the habitual criminal, of course," Prosker said pleasantly, "but this may be the first instance in the history of the world of a habitual crime."

Greenwood leaned over and jabbed Prosker in the ribs. "You keep talking," he said. "Stop it."

The Major said, "One thing I don't understand. Dortmunder, you claim to be sick of this whole business. You had to be persuaded by your friends to join in on this most recent chapter, and the time before that it took a promise of more money per week and a higher payment at the end to induce you to go on. But now, all at once you are prepared to continue with no persuasion, no arguing for more money, no hesitation of any kind. I frankly don't understand it."

"That emerald," Dortmunder said, "is an albatross

around my neck. I used to think I could get away from it, but now I know better. I could walk out of here now, try to find something else to do with my life, but sooner or later that goddamn emerald would pop up again, I'd be right back in the middle of the mess again. When Prosker told us this morning what he'd done with it, I all of a sudden knew it was destiny. Either I get that emerald, or the emerald gets me, and until it happens one way or the other I'm stuck with it. I can't get free, so why fight it?"

"A bank on Fifth Avenue in Manhattan," the Major said, "is a far cry from an upstate sanitarium, or even a Long Island prison."

"I know it," Dortmunder said.

"This could very well be the most difficult job you've ever attempted."

"It definitely is," Dortmunder said. "The New York City banks got the most sophisticated alarm and camera systems in the world, plus grade-A guards, plus plenty of city cops just outside the door. Plus the traffic jam that midtown is always in the middle of, that you can't even make a getaway."

"You know all that," the Major said, "but you still want to go on with it?"

"We all do," Kelp said.

"It's a matter of honor," Murch said. "Like not gettin' passed on the right."

"I want to go on with it," Dortmunder said, "to the point that I want to look over the bank and see is there anything I can do about it. If I can't, then that's it."

The Major said, "You'll want to be on salary while making up your mind, is that it?"

Dortmunder looked at him. "You think I'm here for the two hundred a week?"

"I don't know," the Major said. "By this time, I don't know anything for sure anymore."

Dortmunder said, "I'll give you your answer within one week. If the answer's no, that's only one week's salary you've blown. In fact, Major, just because you're getting me irritated I'll tell you that if the answer's no, for myself I'll give you back the two hundred."

"That's hardly necessary," the Major said. "The two hundred dollars isn't the point."

"Then stop talking as though it is. I'll give you your answer in one week."

"No need to hurry," the Major said. "Take your time. I'm just upset, that's all, just as all of you are upset. For the same reason. And Kelp is right, we shouldn't fight among ourselves."

"Why not?" Prosker asked, smiling at them.

Greenwood leaned over and knuckled Prosker behind the ear. "You're starting up again," he said. "Better don't."

The Major pointed at Prosker and said, "What about him?"

Dortmunder said, "He told us where to find the key in his office, so we don't need him any more. But we can't let him go yet. You got a basement?"

The Major looked surprised. "You want me to hold him for you?"

"Temporarily," Dortmunder said.

Prosker looked at the Major and said, "It's called accessory after the fact."

Greenwood stretched and kicked Prosker on the shin, saying, "When are you gonna learn?"

Prosker turned to him and said, calmly but with some irritation, "Greenwood, stop that."

Greenwood stared at him in astonishment.

The Major said to Dortmunder, "I don't like keeping him here, but I suppose you have no other place."

"That's right."

The Major shrugged. "Very well then."

"We'll see you later," Dortmunder said and started for the door.

"Just a moment," the Major said. "Please wait till I bring in reinforcements. I'd rather not be alone with my prisoner."

"Sure," said Dortmunder, and he and the other four stood clustered near the door while the Major got on his intercom. Prosker sat in the middle of the room, smiling amiably at everybody, his right hand thrust into his bathrobe pocket, and a few minutes later two burly black men came in and saluted the Major, reporting in some foreign tongue.

"I'll be in touch, Major," Dortmunder said.

"Good," the Major said. "I do still have confidence in you, Dortmunder."

Dortmunder grunted and went on out, followed by the other four.

The Major, in his native language, told the two burly men to lock Prosker in the basement. They proceeded to obey, picking Prosker up by the elbows, when Prosker said conversationally to the Major, "A nice bunch of boys, those, but awfully naïve."

"Goodbye, Advocate Prosker," the Major said.

Prosker still looked relaxed and amiable as the burly men started him toward the door. "Do you realize," he said easily, "that it hasn't occurred to even one of them to ask himself if you really intend to pay off when you get the emerald?"

"*Moka!*" said the Major, and the burly men stopped halfway to the door. "*Kamina loba dai,*" said the Major, and the burly men turned Prosker around and carried him back to his chair and sat him down in it. "*Torolima,*" the Major said, and the burly men left the room.

Prosker sat there smiling.

The Major said, "Did you give them any such idea?"

"Of course not," said Prosker.

"Why not?"

"Major," said Prosker, "you are black and I am white. You are a military man and I am an attorney. You are African and I am American. But somehow I sense a kinship between us, Major, that I just don't feel between myself and any of those five worthy gentlemen who just left."

The Major slowly sat down again behind his desk. "What's in it for you, Prosker?" he said.

Prosker smiled again. "I was hoping *you'd* tell *me*, Major," he said.

2

Nine o'clock Wednesday evening, two days after the meeting in Major Iko's office, Dortmunder walked into the O. J. Bar and Grill and nodded to Rollo, who said, "Good to see you again."

"Anybody else here?"

"Everybody except the beer and salt. The other bourbon has your glass."

"Thanks."

Dortmunder walked through to the back room, where Kelp and Greenwood and Chefwick were sitting around the round table under the green-metal-shaded light. The table was covered with indictable evidence of a crime being planned, meaning photographs and sketches and even blueprints of the 46th Street and Fifth Avenue branch of the Capitalists & Immigrants National Bank (whose television mascot was a German shepherd with the slogan "Let C&I be the seeing-eye to all your banking needs").

Dortmunder sat down in front of the empty glass,

exchanged hellos with the others, and poured some bourbon. He drank, put the glass down, and said, "Well? What do you think?"

"Bad," said Kelp.

"Rotten," said Greenwood.

"I agree," said Chefwick. "What do you think, Dortmunder?"

The door opened and Murch came in. Everybody said hello, and he said, "I made a mistake this time." He sat down in the vacant chair and said, "I thought it might be a good idea to take Pennsylvania Avenue to the Interborough, and then Woodhaven Boulevard to Queens Boulevard and the Fifty-ninth Street Bridge, but it didn't work out. You got a lot of bad traffic there, especially on Queens Boulevard, the kind that just mopes along but takes up all the lanes to do it, so you can get caught by the lights a lot. Otherwise I'd of been here ahead of time."

Dortmunder said to him, "The question is, what do you think of this bank job?"

"Well, you're not going to make a getaway," Murch told him, "that's one thing for sure. Now, Forty-sixth Street is one way eastbound, and Fifth Avenue is one way southbound, which gives you only half the usual directions just to begin with. Then there's the problem of traffic lights. There's a traffic light at every intersection in Manhattan, and they're all red. If you go over Forty-sixth toward Madison, you'll get all tied up in the middle of the block somewhere. If you go south on Fifth Avenue, you might be able to keep moving because they've got staggered lights, but even so they're set for something like twenty-two miles an hour, and you just don't make a getaway at twenty-two miles an hour."

Dortmunder said, "What about at night?"

"Less traffic," Murch said, "but just as many lights. And there's always cops around midtown, so you don't want to run any lights, and even if you do you'll get hit by a cab in the first ten blocks. Day or night, you don't make any getaway by car."

Greenwood said, "Helicopter again?"

Kelp answered him, saying, "I thought about that, but it's no good. It's a forty-seven-story building, with the bank on the ground floor. You can't put the helicopter in the street, and if you put it on the roof you've got to make a getaway by elevator, which is also no good, because all the cops have to do is turn off the power to the elevator while we're in it and come collect us like canned sardines."

"Right," Murch said. "There is no method to make a getaway from Forty-sixth Street and Fifth Avenue, and that's all there is to it."

Dortmunder nodded and said to Chefwick, "What about locks?"

Chefwick shook his head. "I haven't been down in the vault," he said, "but just from what I could see up on the main floor they don't have the kind of locks you pick. It would take blasting, probably some drilling. A lot of time, and a lot of noise."

Dortmunder nodded again and looked around at Kelp and Greenwood. "Any suggestions? Any ideas?"

Kelp said, "I thought about going through walls, but it can't be done. You take a look on that blueprint there, you'll see not only is the vault underground, surrounded by rocks and telephone company cable and power lines and water pipes and God knows what all, but the walls are eight-foot-thick reinforced concrete with sensor alarms that ring at the local precinct house."

Greenwood said, "I spent some time working out what would happen if we just walked in and pulled guns and said this is a stick-up. In the first place, we'd get our pictures taken, which any other time is all right with me, but not in the middle of a heist. Also, everybody in the joint has foot alarms under where they work. Also, the downstairs entrance to the vault is always barred shut unless there's somebody going down there on legitimate business, and there's two barred doors with a room in between, and they never have both doors open at the same time. I also think they have other stuff that I'm not sure of. Even if we could work out some kind of getaway, there's no job in there to make a getaway from."

"That's right," Dortmunder said. "I came to the same conclusion as you guys. I just wanted to hear did any of you think of something I missed."

"We didn't," Chefwick said.

"You mean that's it?" Kelp said. "We give it up? The job can't be done?"

"I didn't say that," Dortmunder said. "I didn't say the job couldn't be done. But what we've all said is that none of us could do it. It isn't a place for a frontal attack. We've hit up Iko for trucks, for a helicopter, for a locomotive, I'm sure we could hit him up for just about anything we'd need. But there's nothing he could give us that would do the trick. He could give us a tank and it wouldn't help."

"Because we'd never get away in it," Murch said.

"That's right."

"Though it might be fun to drive one," Murch said thoughtfully.

Kelp said, "Wait a minute. Dortmunder, if you say none of us could pull this job, you're saying the job can't be done. What's the difference? We're shot down whatever way you say it."

"No, we're not," Dortmunder said. "There's five of us here, and none of the five of us could get that emerald out of that bank. But that doesn't mean nobody in the world could do it."

Greenwood said, "You mean bring in somebody new?"

"I mean," Dortmunder said, "bring in a specialist. This time we need a specialist outside the string, so we bring one in."

"What kind of a specialist?" Greenwood said, and Kelp said, "Who?"

"Miasmo the Great," Dortmunder said.

There was a little silence, and then everybody began to smile. "That's nice," Greenwood said.

Kelp said, "You mean for Prosker?"

"I wouldn't trust Prosker," Dortmunder said.

Everybody stopped smiling, and looked baffled instead. Chefwick said, "If not Prosker, who?"

"An employee of the bank," Dortmunder said.

Everybody started smiling again.

3

The Major was leaning over the pool table when Kelp was shown in by the ebony man with the light-reflecting glasses, and Prosker was sitting at his ease in a leather chair to one side. Prosker was no longer dressed in pajamas and bathrobe, but was now wearing a neat business suit and nursing a tall drink that tinkled.

The Major said, "Ah, Kelp! Come watch this, I saw it on television."

Kelp walked over to the pool table. "Do you think it's all right to have him walking around?"

The Major glanced at Prosker, then said, "There's nothing to worry about. Mr. Prosker and I have an understanding. He has given me his word not to try to escape."

"His word and a dime will get you a cup of coffee," Kelp said, "but it tastes better with just the dime."

"Additionally," the Major said casually, "the doors are guarded. Now, really, you must watch this. You see,

I have the cue ball here, and those three balls against that cushion over there, and that ball down at the far end. Now, I will hit the ball on the right end of those three, and all four will go into four different pockets. Do you think that's impossible?"

Kelp, who had seen the same thing on television several times, with a gradually mounting sense of apathy, was sure it was possible, but why spoil the Major's fun? "You'll have to prove it to me, Major," he said.

The Major gave the broad smile of a man who's been practicing and leaned with careful attention over the table. He sighted along the cue, took a few tentative pokes at the cue ball, then struck. Clack-clack-clackety-clack, balls rolled hither and yon. One plopped into a pocket, two more did, and the fourth hit the shoulder, nearly fell in, but decided at the last second to roll the other way.

"Drat!" said the Major.

"That was almost," Kelp said, to make him feel better. "And I can see now the way it would work. That one pretty near fell in."

"I did it before you came," said the Major. "Didn't I, Prosker?"

"Absolutely," said Prosker.

"I believe you," said Kelp.

"I have to show you," the Major said. "Just a moment now, just a moment."

The Major hurriedly set up the trick again. Kelp, glancing at Prosker, saw him giving a small sympathetic smile. Choosing not to accept the comradeship the smile implied, Kelp looked away again.

The Major was ready once more. He urged Kelp to watch, and Kelp said he would. And he did, praying the Major would make it this time, because he was apparently prepared to keep trying all night long if he had to, in order to do it in front of Kelp.

Clack. Clackety-clackety-clack. Ball number one dropped into a pocket, two and three followed, and number four hit the shoulder, teetered on the edge, spun slowly, reluctantly, and fell into the pocket.

The Major and Kelp heaved simultaneous sighs of relief, and the Major put down his cue stick with obvious pleasure to have it done and over with. "Now," he said, rubbing his hands together, "Dortmunder called last night and said he thought there was a way to do it. That was fast work, very fast. You have a list for me?"

"No list this time," Kelp said. "All we need is cash. Five thousand dollars."

The Major stared. "Five thou—" He swallowed and said, "For God's sake, why?"

"We have to hire a specialist," Kelp said. "We can't do this one like the other ones, we need a specialist. He gets a flat fee of five grand. Dortmunder says you can take it off our payments when we give you the emerald because he's an extra man you didn't count on."

The Major glanced at Prosker, then looked at Kelp again. "I wouldn't have that much cash right now," he said. "How soon do you need it?"

"The sooner we get the money," Kelp said, "the sooner the specialist goes to work."

"Who is this specialist?"

"He calls himself Miasmo the Great."

The Major was taken aback. "What on earth does he do?"

Kelp told him.

The Major and Prosker exchanged a quick startled glance, and the Major said, "You mean on Prosker here?"

"No," Kelp said, not noticing how the word made them both relax. "We don't trust Prosker, he might be able to fake it."

"That's good," Prosker said amiably. "Never be too trusting, that's what I say."

The Major gave him a dirty look.

"We'll go for one of the guards of the bank," Kelp said.

"You have a plan, then," the Major said.

"Dortmunder's worked out another dilly."

"I will have the money by two o'clock tomorrow afternoon," the Major said. "Will someone come by for it?"

"Probably me," Kelp said.

"Fine. And you need no other equipment?"

"No, just the five grand."

"Then," said the Major, moving toward the pool table, "let me show you something else I saw—"

"I'd love to see it, Major, I really would," Kelp said quickly, "but the fact of the matter is, I promised Dortmunder I'd come right back. We've got preparations to make, you know, things to get ready for."

The Major paused beside the table, clearly disappointed. "Perhaps when you come for the money tomorrow," he said.

"That's a good idea," Kelp said, making a mental

note to send Murch for the money the next day. "Well, I'll be seeing you, Major. I know my way to the door."

"Until tomorrow," the Major said.

"My best to Greenwood and all the boys," Prosker said cheerfully, and Kelp left the room, closing the door behind him.

The Major turned angrily to Prosker, saying, "You are not amusing."

"They don't suspect a thing," Prosker said easily. "None of them."

"They will if you keep being playful."

"No, they won't. I know where to draw the line."

"Do you?" The Major lit a cigarette with nervous angry movements. "I don't like toying with those people," he said. "It could be dangerous. They could all be very very dangerous."

"That's why you like having me around," Prosker said. "You know I know how to deal with them."

The Major studied him cynically. "Is that why? I wondered why I wasn't keeping you stuffed away in the basement."

"I'm useful, Major," Prosker said.

"We'll see," the Major said. "We'll see."

4

In suit and tie, Dortmunder could look like a slightly seedy small businessman. As though he operated something like a laundromat in a poor neighborhood. It was a good enough appearance to carry him through his errand to the bank.

Today was Friday the thirteenth. A superstitious man might have waited until Monday for this part of the preparation, but Dortmunder was not a superstitious man. He accepted the fact that the Balabomo Emerald was a jinx in a jinxless world, and didn't allow the contradiction to lead him into irrational fears of numbers or dates or black cats or spilled salt or any of the other chimerical goads with which people plague themselves. All other inanimate objects were tame and neutral, only the Balabomo Emerald was possessed of an evil spirit.

Dortmunder walked into the bank a little after two, a relatively quiet period, and walked over to one of the uniformed guards, a slender white-haired man sucking his false teeth. "I want to see about renting a safe deposit box," Dortmunder said.

"You'll want to talk to an officer of the bank," the guard said and escorted Dortmunder over behind a rail.

The officer was a soft young man in a dandruff-flecked tan suit who told Dortmunder the box rental was eight dollars and forty cents a month, and when that didn't seem to stun Dortmunder the young man gave him a form to fill out, full of the usual questions—address, occupation, and so on—which Dortmunder answered with lies prepared for the occasion.

After the paperwork was done, the young man escorted Dortmunder downstairs to look at his box. At the foot of the stairs was a uniformed guard, and the young man explained to Dortmunder the signing-in procedure he would have to follow every time he visited his box. The first gate was then unlocked and they stepped through into a small room where Dortmunder was introduced to a second uniformed guard, who would take over from here. The young man shook Dortmunder's hand, welcomed him once again to C&I's happy family, and went back upstairs.

The new guard, who was named Albert, said, "Either George or I will always serve you, any time you want to get to your box."

"George?"

"He's the one on the sign-in desk today."

Dortmunder nodded.

Albert then unlocked the inner gate and they went through into a room that looked like a Lilliputian morgue, with rank upon rank of trays for the tiny dead bodies.

Buttons of various colors were attached to many of the drawer fronts, each color probably having great significance to the bank.

Dortmunder's drawer was low and to the left. Albert used his own master key first, then asked to borrow the key Dortmunder had just received from the young man upstairs. Dortmunder gave it to him, he unlocked the drawer, and at once gave the key back to Dortmunder.

The safe deposit box was actually a drawer, about an inch high, four inches wide and eighteen inches deep. Albert slid it most of the way out, and said, "If you wish privacy, sir, I can carry it into one of the side rooms for you," motioning to the small chambers off the main morgue, each containing a table and a chair, in which the box holder could at his desire communicate alone with his box.

"No, thanks," Dortmunder said. "I don't need that this time. I just want to put this stuff in." And he took from his inside jacket pocket a bulky sealed white envelope containing seven unused Kleenex tissues. He carefully placed this in the middle of the drawer, and stood back while Albert shut it up again.

Albert let him out the first gate and George let him out the second, and Dortmunder went upstairs and outside, where it seemed strange somehow that it was still daylight. He checked his watch and hailed a cab, because he now had to get uptown and then come all the way back with Miasmo the Great before the bank's employees started going home for the day.

5

"New York is a lonely city, Linda," Greenwood said.

"Oh, it is," she said. "I know that, Alan." He had kept
his first name, and his new last name also started with
G, which was safe enough and very convenient.

Greenwood adjusted the pillow behind his head and
clasped his arm tighter around the girl beside him. "When
one meets a sympathetic soul in a city like this," he said,
"one doesn't want to let go."

"Oh, I know what you mean," she said and snug-
gled more comfortably against him, her cheek resting
against his bare chest, the covers warm over their bodies.

"That's why I hate it that I have to go out tonight,"
he said.

"Oh, I hate it too," she said.

"But how did I know a treasure like you would come
into my life today? And now it's too late to change this
other thing. I just have to go, that's all there is to it."

She lifted her head and studied his face. The artificial fireplace in the corner was the only source of light, and she peered at him in its uncertain red light. "Are you sure it isn't another girl?" she asked. She was trying to make the question light, but wasn't entirely succeeding.

He cupped her chin in his hand. "There is no other girl," he said. "Not anywhere in the world." He kissed her lightly on the lips.

"I do want to believe you, Alan," she said. She looked sweet, and plaintive, and yearning.

"And I wish I was permitted to tell you where I am going," he said, "but I can't. I just ask you to trust me. And I should be back in no more than an hour."

She smiled, saying, "You couldn't do very much with another girl in an hour, could you?"

"Not when I want to save myself for you," he said and kissed her again.

After the kiss she murmured in his ear, "How much time do we have before you go?"

He had been squinting at the bedside clock over her shoulder, and he said, "Twenty minutes."

"Then there's time," she murmured, nibbling his ear, "to make doubly sure you won't forget me."

"Mmmmmm," he said, and the result was that when the doorbell sounded, one long, two short, one long, twenty minutes later, he wasn't finished dressing. "There they are," he said, tugging on his trousers.

"Hurry back to me, Alan," she said. She was stretching and wriggling under the covers.

He watched the covers moving and said, "Oh, I'll

hurry, Linda. Don't you worry, I'll hurry." He kissed her, put on his jacket, and left the apartment.

Chefwick was waiting on the sidewalk. "You were quite some time," he said, gently chiding.

"You don't know the half of it," Greenwood said. "Which way?"

"This way."

Murch was at the wheel of his Mustang around the corner, parked by a fire hydrant. Chefwick and Greenwood got into the car, Chefwick in back, and Murch drove downtown to Varick Street, where all the office buildings had been shut down for hours. He parked across the street from the one they wanted, and Greenwood and Chefwick got out and went across the street. Greenwood stood watch while Chefwick opened the front door, and then they went in and up the stairs—the elevators not working now—to the fifth floor. They went down the hall, Greenwood lighting their way with a small pencil flash, until they found the door marked DODSON & FOGG, ATTORNEYS AT LAW. On the lower left corner of the frosted glass were five names, of which the second was E. ANDREW PROSKER.

Chefwick went through this door so fast it might as well not have been locked at all. Now they followed the map Prosker had drawn for them, finding Prosker's office amid the maze of cubbyholes, finding the furniture arranged as Prosker had said. Greenwood sat down at the desk, opened the bottom right-hand drawer all the way, and to the back was taped a small yellow envelope. Greenwood smiled and took the envelope and put the drawer back. He shook the envelope over the desk pad and a small key dropped out, looking exactly like the one Dortmunder had been given at the bank earlier today.

"We've got it," Greenwood said. "Isn't that amazing?"

"Perhaps our luck has changed," Chefwick said.

"And it's Friday the thirteenth. Fantastic."

"Not any longer, it's after midnight."

"It is? Let's go. Here, you'll give this to Dortmunder."

Chefwick put the key in his pocket and they left the office, Chefwick relocking doors on their route back to the street and Murch. They got in and Greenwood said, "Would you mind dropping me first? I've got a little something going on back at my place."

"It's perfectly all right with me," Chefwick said.

"Sure," said Murch. "Why not?"

They drove back uptown and let Greenwood off in front of his building and he took the elevator up to his apartment, where he found the girl sitting up in bed and reading a paperback James Bond book. She put the book away at once and switched off the bedside lamp, while Greenwood got rid of a lot of extraneous clothing and got back into bed beside her.

Softly she said, "Did everything go all right?"

"I'm back," he said simply.

She kissed his chest and looked up at him wickedly. "You're in the CIA, aren't you?" she said.

"I'm not allowed to talk about it," he said.

"Mmmmmm," she said and began to bite him all over.

"I love patriotic women," Greenwood murmured.

6

Thursday, the nineteenth of October, was one of those changeable days. It started off with a drenching rain in the morning, then turned windy and cold, then the clouds blew away in the middle of the afternoon and the sun came out, and by five-thirty it was as warm as a summer afternoon. Albert Cromwell, safe deposit box guard at the 46th Street and Fifth Avenue branch of C&I National Bank, had worn raincoat and rubbers in the morning as well as carrying an umbrella, and went home carrying all three. He didn't know whether to be disgusted at the changeableness of the weather or pleased with the goodness it had finally arrived at, and decided to be both.

Home for Albert Cromwell was a twenty-seventh-story apartment in a thirty-five-story building on the Upper West Side, and he traveled there by subway and elevator. Today, as he entered the elevator on the final leg of his homeward journey, a tall and imposing man with piercing black eyes, a broad forehead, and thick hair jet black everywhere except for the gray at the temples boarded with him. Albert Cromwell hadn't noticed, but the same man had entered the elevator with him every evening this week, the only difference today being that this was the first time the two of them were alone.

They stood side by side, Albert Cromwell and the imposing man, both facing front. The doors slid shut and the elevator began to rise.

"Have you ever noticed those numbers?" the imposing man said. He had a deep and resonant voice.

Albert Cromwell looked at the other man in surprise. Strangers didn't talk to one another in the elevator. He said, "I beg your pardon?"

The imposing man nodded at the row of numbers over the door. "I mean those numbers there," he said. "Take a look at them," he suggested.

Puzzled, Albert Cromwell took a look at them. They were small glass numbers running from left to right in a long chrome strip over the door, starting with B at the left (for basement), then L for lobby, then 2, 3, and so on all the way up to 35. The numbers lit up one at a time to indicate which floor the elevator was at. Right now, for instance, the number 4 was on. As Albert Cromwell watched, that number switched off and number 5 switched on in its place.

"Notice how regular the movement is," the imposing man said in his resonant voice. "How pleasant it is to see something so smooth and regular, to count the numbers, to know that each number will follow the one before it. So smooth. So regular. So restful. Watch the numbers. Count along with them, if you wish, it's very restful after a long hard day. It's good to be able to rest, to be able to look at the numbers and count them and feel one's body relaxing, to know that one is relaxing, to know that one is safe in one's own building, safe and relaxed and calm, watching the numbers, counting the numbers, feeling every muscle relax, every nerve relax, knowing that one can now let go, one can lean back against the wall and relax, relax, relax. There's nothing but the numbers now, nothing but the numbers and my voice. Nothing but the numbers and my voice. The numbers and my voice."

The imposing man stopped talking and looked at Albert Cromwell, who was leaning back against the rear wall of the elevator, gazing in a bovine way at the numbers over the door. The number 12 switched off and the number 14 switched on. Albert Cromwell watched the numbers.

The imposing man said, "Can you hear my voice?"

"Yes," said Albert Cromwell.

"One day soon," the imposing man said, "a man will come to you at your place of employment. At the bank where you work. Do you understand me?"

"Yes," said Albert Cromwell.

"The man will say to you, 'Afghanistan banana stand.' Do you understand me?"

"Yes," said Albert Cromwell.

"What will the man say?"

"Afghanistan banana stand," said Albert Cromwell.

"Very good," said the imposing man. The number 17 lit briefly over the door. "You are still very relaxed," said the imposing man. "When the man says to you,

'Afghanistan banana stand,' you will do what he tells you to do. Do you understand me?"

"Yes," said Albert Cromwell.

"What will you do when the man says to you, 'Afghanistan banana stand'?"

"I will do what he tells me to do," said Albert Cromwell.

"Very good," said the imposing man. "That's very good, you're doing very well. When the man leaves you, you will forget that he was there. Do you understand?"

"Yes," said Albert Cromwell.

"What will you do when he leaves you?"

"I will forget he was there," said Albert Cromwell.

"Excellent," said the imposing man. The number 22 lit over the door. "You are doing fine," said the imposing man. He reached out and pushed the button for the twenty-sixth floor. "When I leave you," he said, "you will forget our conversation. When you reach your floor, you will feel rested and very, very good. You will forget our conversation, and you will feel rested and very, very good. You will not remember our conversation until the man says to you, 'Afghanistan banana stand.' Then you will do what he tells you, and after he leaves, you will again forget our conversation and you will also forget that he was ever there. Will you do all that?"

"Yes," said Albert Cromwell.

The number 26 lit over the door, and the elevator came to a stop. The door slid open. "You did very well," the imposing man said, stepping out to the corridor. "Very well," he said, and the door slid shut again, and the elevator went up one more story to the twenty-seventh floor, which was where Albert Cromwell lived. It stopped there, and the door opened, and Albert Cromwell shook himself and stepped out to the hall. He smiled. He felt very good, very relaxed and rested. He walked down the hall with a buoyant step, feeling great, and thinking it must be because of the unseasonably warm weather this afternoon. Whatever it was, he felt great.

7

Dortmunder walked into the bank, remembering what Miasmo the Great had told him last night when reporting success at last with Albert Cromwell. "If at all possible," he had said, "do your work tomorrow. If you miss tomorrow, you'll have the whole weekend to wait before you can try again. The suggestion should be firmly enough fixed to last until Monday, but naturally the sooner you trigger him the better. He could watch a television program Saturday night and somebody on it would say, 'Afghanistan banana stand,' and the whole thing would open up in his mind. So if you can do it tomorrow, do it tomorrow."

So here it was tomorrow. Tomorrow afternoon, in fact. Dortmunder had come here once already today, at nine-thirty this morning, but when he'd walked by the stairway and looked down, it was Albert on duty outside, which meant George would be inside, and George they didn't have primed, so he'd gone away again, coming back now in the hope that Albert and George shifted after lunch and didn't keep the same posts all day long.

Luck was in. Dortmunder got to the head of the stairs and looked down and there was George. Dortmunder didn't hesitate, he trotted down the stairs, said hello to George, signed in, and was let through the first door.

There was no one in the small in-between room, and for just a second Dortmunder felt the cold touch of apprehension in the middle of his back. He could see himself locked away in here by a gloating George, everything known, he being held here until the police could arrive. A fitting end to the Balabomo Emerald quest.

But then George said, "Albert will be with you in just one moment, sir," and Dortmunder's paranoia faded like mist. He nodded, and George shut the barred gate after him and went back over to his desk.

There were a couple of chairs in this room, but Dortmunder was too nerved up to sit down. He stood where he was, as though he'd been left behind by somebody, like an umbrella, and after a couple of minutes the farther door opened and a stout elderly lady emerged, clutching a Pekingese to her fox, and followed by Albert.

Albert shut the gate and said to Dortmunder, "Just one moment, sir."

"Take your time," Dortmunder said.

Albert opened the other gate and let the lady out, then turned to Dortmunder. "If you'll follow me, sir."

They went through the inner gate and directly to Dortmunder's box. Albert inserted his key, asked to borrow Dortmunder's, opened the box, and at once gave Dortmunder his key back.

"I just wanted this," Dortmunder said, and took out the envelope full of tissues. He tucked it away in his inside jacket pocket.

Albert used the two keys to lock the now-empty box, gave Dortmunder back his key, and said, "This way, sir."

"Afghanistan banana stand," Dortmunder said.

Albert stopped where he was. He turned to Dortmunder, and he looked calmly prepared to be of service. "Yes, sir," he said.

Dortmunder took out Prosker's key. "Now we'll open this box," he said.

"Yes, sir." Albert took the key and turned away. Dortmunder followed him, and they walked down the aisle to Prosker's box. Albert used the two keys and opened the box, then stood there continuing to look calm and alert and ready to be of service.

There were a lot of papers in Prosker's box, deeds and thick white envelopes and birth certificates and one thing and another. In with all the rest was a small black plush box of the kind cuff links and earrings come in. Dortmunder reached into the drawer, picked up the black plush box, and opened it.

The Balabomo Emerald. Filling the little box and winking at Dortmunder under the fluorescent lights. Grinning to itself inside the little box.

Dortmunder shut the little box again and slipped it into his left-side jacket pocket. He said to Albert, "All right, shut it up again."

"Yes, sir."

Albert shut the drawer and gave Dortmunder Prosker's key. He then went back to looking alert, calm, ready to serve.

Dortmunder said, "That's all. I'm ready to leave now."

"Yes, sir."

Albert led the way to the first gate, opened it, stood aside for Dortmunder to go on through. Then Dortmunder had to wait while he closed it again before crossing the small anteroom and opening the outer gate. Dortmunder walked past him, and outside George said, "Have a good day, sir."

"Thank you," Dortmunder said. He went upstairs and out of the bank and caught a cab. "Amsterdam Avenue and Eighty-fourth Street," he said.

The cab went down 45th Street and turned right and got itself snarled in a traffic jam. Dortmunder sat in the back and slowly began to smile. It was incredible. They had the emerald. They actually had the emerald, at long last. Dortmunder saw the cabby puzzling at him in the rearview mirror, wondering what a passenger caught in a traffic jam had to smile about, but he couldn't stop. He just went right on smiling.

PHASE
SIX

PHASE
SIX

1

Around the table in the back room at the O. J. Bar and Grill sat Murch and Kelp and Chefwick. Murch was drinking beer and salt and Kelp was drinking straight bourbon, but since it was barely midafternoon Chefwick was not drinking his usual sherry. Instead he was having a Diet-Rite Cola, and he was nursing it. Greenwood was out in the bar, showing Rollo how to make a vodka sour on the rocks, and Rollo was watching with a skeptical frown and managing to remember none of the details.

The three in the back room had been silent five or six minutes when Murch suddenly said, "You know, I've been thinking about it."

"That's a mistake," Kelp said. "Don't think about it. It'll give you a rash."

"I've been sitting here," Murch persisted, "and I've been trying to think what could possibly go wrong this time. Like maybe they moved the bank since yesterday.

Like somebody that works there embezzled the emerald."

Chefwick said quietly, "I agree with Kelp. I think you should stop thinking about it at once. Or at least stop talking about it."

Murch said, "But they don't sound right. There's nothing I can think of that sounds like the kind of snafu that happens to us. I'm almost ready to believe Dortmunder is actually going to walk through that door over there with the emerald in his hand." Murch pointed at the door, and it opened, and Greenwood walked in with the vodka sour in his hand. He blinked mildly at the finger Murch was pointing at him and said, "Somebody calling me?"

Murch stopped pointing. "No," he said. "I was just saying I was optimistic, that's all."

"Mistake," Greenwood commented and sat down at the table. "I very carefully left this evening open," he said, "on the assumption we'd all be sitting around this room tonight working out the next caper."

"Don't even say that," said Kelp.

Greenwood shook his head. "If I say it, it might not happen," he said. "But what if I'd called some beautiful and willing young lady and arranged to cook dinner for her at my place tonight? What then, Kelp?"

"Yeah," said Kelp. "You're right."

"Exactly." Greenwood tasted his vodka sour. "Mmm. Very good."

"This is a nice place," Murch agreed. "It's kind of far from my neighborhood, though, to just drop in.

Though if I'm on the Belt anyway, or Grand Central, why not." He sipped at his beer and added a little salt.

Kelp said, "What time is it?" but as Chefwick looked at his watch Kelp added quickly, "Don't tell me! I don't want to know."

Greenwood said, "If he does get picked up, if Dortmunder does, we'll have to spring him, of course. The way you guys sprang me."

"Naturally," said Chefwick, and the other two nodded agreement.

"Whether he's got the stone or not, I mean," Greenwood said.

"Sure," said Kelp. "What else?"

Greenwood sighed. "When my dear mother told me to settle down to a steady job," he said, "I really doubt this is what she had in mind."

Murch said, "You think we'll ever really get that stone? Maybe God wants us to go straight, and this is kind of a gentle hint."

"If five jobs for the same emerald is a gentle hint," Kelp said bitterly, "I don't want Him to shout at me."

"Still," said Chefwick, studying his Diet-Rite Cola, "it has been interesting. My first helicopter ride, for instance. And driving Tom Thumb, that was rather pleasant."

"No more interesting jobs," Murch said. "If it's all the same to everybody, I want things dull from now on. All I want is that door should open and Dortmunder should walk in with the emerald in his hand." He pointed at the door again, and it opened again, and Dortmunder walked in with an empty glass in his hand.

Everybody stared at him. Dortmunder stared at the finger pointing at him, then moved out of its line of fire and walked around the table to the vacant chair and the bourbon bottle. He sat down, poured bourbon into his glass, and took a swallow. Everybody watched, un-blinking. The silence was so pure he could be heard swallowing.

He looked around at them. His face was expres-sionless, and so were theirs. Then Dortmunder smiled.

2

The emerald lay in the middle of the scarred wooden table, looking like a beautiful egg laid by the green-metal-shaded hanging light directly overhead. That light was reflected and refracted a thousand times in the prisms of the stone, so that the emerald looked as though it were silently laughing and chuckling and giggling in the middle of the table there. Happy to be the center of attention. Happy to be so much admired.

The five men sitting around the table stared at the emerald for some time, as though expecting pictures of their future to form in its facets. The outside world was far away, faint dim traffic sounds from another planet. The silence in the back room at the O. J. Bar and Grill was both reverential and ecstatic. The five men had an air of awed solemnity about them, and yet they were all smiling. From ear to ear. Gazing at the winking, laughing stone and smiling back at it.

Kelp sighed. He said, "There it is."

The others shifted position, as though waking from a trance. Murch said, "I never thought it would happen."

"But there she is," Greenwood said. "And isn't she a beauty."

"I wish Maude could see that," Chefwick said. "I should have brought my Polaroid to take a picture of it."

"I almost hate to get rid of it," Kelp said.

Dortmunder nodded and said, "I know what you mean. We went through so much for that rock. But we got to get rid of it, and right away. That stone's made me too jumpy. I keep thinking any second that door over there is going to open and a million cops run in."

"They're all downtown beating up children," Greenwood said.

"Nevertheless," Dortmunder said, "the time has come to turn that rock over to Major Iko and collect our money."

Murch said, "You want us all to go? I got my car."

"No," Dortmunder said. "The five of us together might attract attention. Besides, if something goes wrong there should at least be some of us still on the loose and ready to help. Kelp, this was your job first, you brought the rest of us into it, you were the first one the Major contacted. And you're the one that's been bringing him the lists and things all along. You want to bring him the stone?"

"Sure," Kelp said. He was pleased. "If you guys all think I can make it across town."

"Murch can drive you," Dortmunder said, "and we three'll stay here. And if the jinx hits again, it would have hit no matter who was carrying the stone. If it gets you, we'll understand."

Kelp wasn't sure if that was reassuring or not, and while he sat there frowning about it Dortmunder picked up the emerald and put it back into its little black plush box. He handed it to Kelp, who took it and said, "If we're not back in an hour, God knows where we are."

"We'll wait till we hear from you," Dortmunder said. "After you go, I'll call the Major and tell him to open his safe."

"Good." Kelp put the little box away in his pocket, finished his bourbon, and got to his feet. "Come on, Murch."

"Wait'll I finish my beer," Murch said. He was having trouble taking big swallows. Finally he emptied the glass and got to his feet. "Ready," he said.

"See you later," Kelp said to the others and went out. Murch followed him, and the others heard him saying, "The question is, do we go through the park at Sixty-fifth Street, or—" And the door closed.

Dortmunder had to borrow a dime. Chefwick gave him one, and he went out front to the phone booth and called the embassy. He had to talk to two other people before Iko at last got on the phone, and then he said, "We're making delivery this afternoon."

"Are you really?" The Major was obviously delighted. "That is good news. I'd about given up hope."

"So had we all, Major. You understand it's COD."

"Naturally. I have the money waiting in the safe."

"The usual guy is bringing it."

"Not all of you?" The Major sounded disappointed.

"I didn't like the idea of traveling in a bunch. It could get us the wrong kind of attention."

"I suppose so," the Major said dubiously. "Well, it will all work out, I'm sure. Thank you for calling. I'll be expecting our friend."

"Good," Dortmunder said. He hung up and left the booth.

Rollo looked over at him as he started for the back room again and said, "You're lookin' cheerful today."

"It's a cheerful day," Dortmunder said. "Looks like we won't be using your back room any more for a while."

"Mazeltov," Rollo said.

"Yeah," Dortmunder said, and went into the back room to wait.

3

The usual ebony man with the light-reflecting glasses let Kelp in, but he did not lead him toward the usual room. "Hey," Kelp said when they made the wrong turning. "Pool table, remember?" He made motions of waggling a cue.

"Office today," the ebony man said.

"Oh? Yeah, I guess today is special. Okay, lead on." Besides, Kelp was just as relieved that the Major wouldn't have the chance to show him any more tricks he'd learned.

Or would he? The ebony man opened the office door and Kelp went inside and the Major wasn't sitting behind the desk at all. Prosker was, sitting there as though he owned the joint, smiling amiably at Kelp like a spider smiling at a fly.

Kelp stopped just past the door, but a hand in the middle of his back pushed him on. "Hey!" he said and turned around, and the ebony man had come in after him, had shut the door, had drawn an automatic from his pocket, and was pointing it at Kelp's nose.

Kelp stepped backward farther into the room, putting more air between himself and the nozzle of that automatic. "What's going on here?" he said, and now he saw two more black men with guns in their hands, standing against the back wall.

Prosker chuckled.

Kelp whirled and glared at him. "What'd you do with the Major?"

Prosker broke up entirely. "With the *Major*! Oh, my God! You people are babes in the woods, babes in the woods! What did I do with the Major!"

Kelp took a threatening step forward. "Yeah, what did you do with the Major. What are you up to?"

"I am speaking for the Major," Prosker said, sobering. He rested his hands easily on the desktop. "I am working for the Major now," he said, "and the Major thought it would be better if I took over the task of explaining the facts of life to you. He thought the legal mind would better be able to sum the whole matter up in a few sentences that you could then take back with you to your friends. Besides, I made up a good deal of the plot myself."

"Plot?" Kelp could feel those three guns burning little holes in the back of his neck, but he was damned if he'd show anything but self-confidence and anger. "What plot?" he demanded.

"Sit down, Kelp," Prosker offered. "We'll talk."

"We won't talk," Kelp said. "I'll talk to the Major."

Prosker's smile turned, became saddened. "Do I have

to ask the people behind you to force you to sit down? Wouldn't you rather we handled all this without violence?"

Kelp thought it over, then said, "All right, I'll listen. All it is is words so far." He sat down.

"Words is all you're going to get, I'm afraid," said Prosker, "so listen to them carefully. In the first place, you are going to turn the Balabomo Emerald over to me, and you are not going to get any more money for it. The Major has paid you all a total of fourteen thousand three hundred dollars, plus five thousand for that hypnotist, plus nearly five thousand in other expenses, making over twenty-four thousand dollars he has paid out, which he considers quite enough."

"For a half-million-dollar stone," Kelp said bitterly.

"Which really belongs to the Major's nation anyway," Prosker pointed out. "Twenty-four thousand dollars is a lot of money for a small emerging nation like Talabwo, particularly when it's paid out for the return of their own property."

"Am I supposed to be feeling sorry for Talabwo?" Kelp asked. "I'm being hijacked, my partners and me are getting cheated out of two hundred thousand bucks, and you want me to feel sorry for some country in Africa?"

"I simply want you to understand the situation," Prosker said. "First, I want you to understand why the Major feels justified in making no more payments for the return of his nation's property. I believe I have covered that point now, and will go on to the second. Which is, the Major would prefer it if you and the others did not cause any trouble about this."

"Oh, would he?" Kelp smiled with half his mouth. "That's gonna be tough on the Major," he said.

"Not necessarily," said Prosker. "You recall the Major's passion for dossiers."

Kelp frowned. "Papers in folders," he said. "So what?"

"A lot depends," Prosker said, "on who opens those folders and reads those papers. The Manhattan DA, for instance, would find the dossiers on you five fascinating reading. It would solve five rather spectacular crimes of recent vintage, for one thing, as well as giving him some broad hints about other unsolved crimes in the past."

Kelp squinted at Prosker. "The Major's going to fink on us?"

"Only if you cause trouble," Prosker said. He sat back and spread his hands. "After all," he said, "you all made out rather well, considering how ineptly you handled the assignment."

"Ineptly!"

"It took you five tries to do the job right," Prosker reminded him. He held up a hand to forestall Kelp's sputtering objections, saying, "No one's criticizing. All's well that ends well, as the Bard once put it, and you and your friends did finally deliver. But you certainly weren't the models of efficiency and professionalism the Major thought he was hiring."

"He intended this doublecross from the beginning," Kelp said angrily.

"I have no opinion on that," Prosker said. "Please put the emerald on this desk now."

"You don't think I was crazy enough to bring it with me, do you?"

"Yes, I do," Prosker said, unruffled. "The question is, are you crazy enough to force those gentlemen behind you to force you to give it up. Are you?"

Kelp thought it over, angrily and bitterly, and decided he wasn't. There was no point bringing unnecessary lumps on oneself. One merely conceded the round, consoling oneself with the thought that the fight wasn't over. Kelp reached into his pocket, took out the black plush box, and put it on the desk.

"Very good," Prosker said, smiling at the box. He reached out both hands, opened the box, smiled at its contents. He shut the box and looked past Kelp at the three silent enforcers. "One of you should take this to the Major," he said.

The ebony man came forward, the light reflecting from his glasses, and took the box. Kelp watched him walk out of the room.

Prosker said, "Now," and Kelp turned his head to look at him again. "Now," Prosker repeated, "here is what is going to happen. Shortly, I am going to leave here and turn myself over to the police. I have a cock-and-bull story worked out about how I was kidnaped by a group that had the mistaken impression I knew where a former client's booty was hidden. It took them several days to accept their mistake, and then they let me go. I didn't recognize any of them, and I don't expect to see any of their pictures in the rogues' gallery. Neither the

Major nor I, you see, are interested in causing you people any unnecessary difficulty. We hope you'll bear that in mind and not force us to harsher steps."

"Get on with it," Kelp said. "What else?"

"Nothing else," Prosker said. "You have been paid all you will be paid. The Major and I have taken it upon ourselves to cover you for your crimes in regard to the emerald. If you now go on about your own business, all five of you, that can be the end of it, but if any of you cause any trouble for either the Major or myself we are in a position to make life very, very difficult for all of you."

"The Major can go back to Talabwo," Kelp pointed out. "But you'll still be around here."

"As a matter of fact, I won't," Prosker said, smiling amiably. "Talabwo has an opening for a legal adviser in reference to their new constitution. A well-paying job, actually, with a subsidy from the United States Government. It should take about five years to get the new constitution ready for ratification. I'm looking forward to the change of scenery."

"I'd like to suggest a change of scenery for you," Kelp said.

"Undoubtedly," agreed Prosker. He glanced at his watch. "I hate to rush you," he said, "but I am a bit pressed for time. Do you have any questions?"

"None you'd like to answer," Kelp said. He got to his feet. "See you around, Prosker," he said.

"I doubt it," Prosker said. "Those two gentlemen will see you to the door."

They did, keeping Kelp in the middle, and closed the door firmly behind him once he was outside.

Murch's car was just around the corner. Kelp ran around and slid into the front seat. Murch said, "Everything okay?"

"Everything stinks," Kelp said quickly. "Pull up to where you can see around the corner."

Murch acted at once, starting the engine and pulling the car forward as he said, "What's the problem?"

"Doublecross. I have to make a phone call. If anybody comes out of that embassy before I get back, run him down."

"Right," said Murch, and Kelp jumped out of the car again.

4

Rollo walked into the back room and said, "The other bourbon's on the phone. He wants to talk to you."

"I knew it," Greenwood said. "Something had to go wrong."

"Maybe not," Dortmunder said, but his face showed he didn't believe it. He got up and followed Rollo out to the bar and hurried down to the phone booth. He slid in, shut the door, picked up the receiver, and said, "Yeah?"

"Cross," Kelp's voice said. "Come over quick."

"Done," Dortmunder said and hung up. He left the booth and hurried toward the back room, calling to Rollo on the way by, "We'll be back soon."

"Sure," Rollo said. "Any time."

Dortmunder opened the back room door, stuck his head in, and said, "Come on."

"This is really irritating," Chefwick said. He banged

his glass of Diet-Rite Cola on the table and followed Dortmunder and Greenwood out of the bar.

They got a cab right away, but it took forever to get through the park. Anyway, it seemed forever. Still, forever ended, and so did the cab ride, with Dortmunder and the others piling out at the corner half a block from the Talabwo embassy. Murch came trotting over as the cab went away, and Dortmunder said, "What's going on?"

"Doublecross," Murch said. "Prosker and the Major are in it together."

"We should have buried him in the woods," Greenwood said. "I knew it at the time, I was just too softhearted."

"Shut up," Dortmunder told him. He said to Murch, "Where's Kelp?"

"Followed them," Murch said. "About five minutes ago, the Major and Prosker and three others came out and took a cab. They had luggage. Kelp's after them in another cab."

"Damn," Dortmunder said. "It took too long to get through the park."

"Are we supposed to wait here for Kelp," Greenwood asked, "or what?"

Murch pointed at a glass-sided phone booth on the opposite corner. "He took that phone number," he said. "He'll call us when he gets the chance."

"Good thinking," Dortmunder said. "All right. Murch, you stay with the phone booth. Chefwick, you and me are going into the embassy. Greenwood, you got your gun on you?"

"Sure."

"Pass it over."

They stood close together briefly, and Greenwood passed over his Terrier. Dortmunder tucked it away in his jacket pocket and said to Greenwood, "You stay outside and watch. Come on."

Murch went back to the phone booth, and Dortmunder and Chefwick and Greenwood hurried up the block to the embassy. Greenwood stopped and leaned against the ornamental iron railing and casually lit a cigarette while Dortmunder and Chefwick went up the stone stoop, Chefwick taking several small slender tools from his pockets as they went.

It was nearly four o'clock on a Friday afternoon, and Fifth Avenue was full of traffic; cabs and buses and occasional private cars and here and there a black limousine all crept southward, a sluggish stream heading down Fifth Avenue with the park on its right and the impressive old stone buildings on its left. The sidewalks were busy too, with nannies walking baby carriages and elevator operators walking dachshunds and colored nurses walking bent old men. Dortmunder and Chefwick kept their backs to it all, shielding Chefwick's busy hands as he went through the door like a car with Platformate going through a paper hoop. The door *ponged* open, and Dortmunder and Chefwick stepped quickly inside, Dortmunder drawing the revolver while Chefwick shut the door again.

The first two rooms they went through, making quick searches, were empty, but the third contained two typewriters and two black female typists. They were quickly tucked away in a closet with a bolt lock, and Dortmunder and Chefwick went on.

In Major Iko's office they found a note pad on the desk, with a pencil notation on the top sheet: "Kennedy—Flight 301—7:15." Chefwick said, "That must be where they're going."

"But what airline?"

Chefwick looked surprised. He studied the note again. "It doesn't say."

"Phone book," Dortmunder said. "Yellow pages."

They both opened drawers, and the Manhattan yellow pages were in the bottom desk drawer on the left. Chefwick said, "Are you going to call every airline?"

"I hope not. Let's try PanAm." He looked up the number, dialed, and after fourteen rings a pleasant but plastic female voice answered. Dortmunder said, "I have what may sound like a stupid question, but I'm trying to prevent an elopement."

"An elopement, sir?"

"I hate to stand in the way of young love," Dortmunder said, "but we've just found out the man is already married. We know they're taking a flight out of Kennedy tonight at seven-fifteen. It's flight three-o-one."

"Is that a PanAm flight, sir?"

"We don't know. We don't know which airline, and we don't know where they're headed."

The office door opened, and the ebony man walked in, white light glinting from his glasses. Dortmunder said into the phone, "Hold on a second." He put the mouthpiece against his chest and showed Greenwood's revolver to the ebony man. "Stand over there," he said, pointing to a bare stretch of wall far from the doorway.

The ebony man put his hands up and walked over to the bare stretch of wall.

Dortmunder kept his eyes and gun on the ebony man, and spoke into the phone again. "I'm sorry. The girl's mother is hysterical."

"Sir, all you have is the flight number and time of departure?"

"And that it's out of Kennedy, yes."

"This may take a little while, sir."

"I'm willing to wait."

"I'll be as fast as I can, sir. Will you hold on?"

"Of course."

There was a click, and Dortmunder said to Chefwick, "Search him."

"Certainly." Chefwick searched the ebony man, and came up with a Beretta Jetfire .25-caliber automatic, a small nasty gun Kelp had already seen a little earlier in the day.

"Tie him up," Dortmunder said.

"My idea exactly," Chefwick said. He said to the ebony man, "Give me your tie and your shoelaces."

"You will fail," the ebony man said.

Dortmunder said, "If he prefers to be shot, stick your gun in his belly to muffle the sound."

"Naturally," Chefwick said.

"I will cooperate," the ebony man said, starting to remove his tie. "But it doesn't matter. You will fail."

Dortmunder held the phone to his ear and the gun pointed at the ebony man, who gave his tie and shoelaces to Chefwick, who said, "Now remove your shoes and socks and lie face down on the floor."

"It does not matter what you do to me," the ebony man said. "I am unimportant, and you will fail."

"If you don't hurry," Dortmunder said, "you'll get even more unimportant."

The ebony man sat down on the floor and took off his shoes and socks, then turned to lie face down. Chefwick used one shoelace to tie his thumbs behind his back, the other to tie his big toes together, and stuffed the tie into the ebony man's mouth.

Chefwick was just finishing up when Dortmunder heard another click, and the female voice said, "Phew. Well, I found it, sir."

"I really appreciate this," Dortmunder said.

"It's an Air France flight to Paris," she said. "That's the only flight with that number leaving at that time."

"Thank you very much," Dortmunder said.

"It's really very romantic, isn't it, sir?" she said. "Eloping to Paris."

"I guess it is," Dortmunder said.

"It's really too bad he's already married."

"These things happen," Dortmunder said. "Thanks again."

"Any time we can be of service, sir."

Dortmunder hung up and said to Chefwick, "Air France to Paris." He got to his feet. "Help me drag that bird around here behind the desk. We don't want anybody finding him and letting him go so he can call the Major at Kennedy."

They toted the ebony man around behind the desk

and left the embassy without seeing anyone else. Green-wood was still loafing around out front, leaning against the iron railing. He fell in with them, and Dortmunder told him what they'd learned as they walked back to the corner and across the street to where Murch was sitting in the phone booth. There Dortmunder said, "Chefwick, you stay here. When Kelp calls, tell him we're on our way and he can leave a message for us at Air France. If they've gone someplace other than Kennedy, you wait here, and when we don't get any message at Air France we'll call you."

Chefwick nodded. "That's fine," he said.

"We'll all meet at the O. J. when this is over," Dort-munder said. "In case we get separated, that's where we'll meet."

"This may be a late night," Chefwick said. "I'd best call Maude."

"Don't tie up that phone."

"Oh, I won't. Good luck."

"Wouldn't that be nice," Dortmunder said. "Come on, Murch, let's see how fast you can get us to Ken-nedy Airport."

"Well, from here," Murch said, as they trotted across the street toward his car, "I'm going to go straight up FDR Drive to the Triborough . . ."

5

The girl at the Air France counter had a French accent. "Mister Dortmun-dair?" she said. "Yes, I have a message for you." She handed over a small envelope.

"Thank you," Dortmunder said, and he and Greenwood moved away from the counter. Murch was out parking the car. Dortmunder opened the envelope and inside was a small piece of paper containing the scrawled words "Golden Door."

Dortmunder turned the paper over, and the other side was blank. He turned it back and it still said "Golden Door." That's all, just "Golden Door." "I needed this," Dortmunder said.

"Just a minute," Greenwood said and walked over to the nearest passing stewardess, a pretty short-haired blonde in a dark blue uniform. "Excuse me," Greenwood said, "will you marry me?"

"I'd love to," she said, "but my plane leaves in twenty minutes."

"When you come back," Greenwood said. "In the meantime, could you tell me what and where is the Golden Door?"

"Oh, that's the restaurant in the International Arrivals Building."

"Lovely. When can we have dinner there?"

"Oh, the next time you're in town," she said.

"Wonderful," he said. "When will that be?"

"Don't you know?"

"Not yet. When do you get back?"

"Monday," she said, smiling. "We come in at three-thirty in the afternoon."

"A perfect time for dinner. Shall we make it four?"

"Make it four-thirty."

"Four-thirty Monday, at the Golden Door. I'll reserve the table immediately. Under the name of Grofield," he said, giving his most recent name.

"I'll be there," she said. She had a lovely smile and lovely teeth.

"See you then," Greenwood said and went back over to Dortmunder. "It's a restaurant, in the International Arrivals Building."

"Come on."

They went outside, and met Murch on his way in. They brought him up to date, asked a luggage handler to point out the International Arrivals Building, and took the bus over.

The Golden Door is upstairs, at the head of a long broad escalator. At the foot of it stood Kelp. Dortmunder and the other two went over, and Kelp said, "They're up there feeding their faces."

"They're taking the seven-fifteen Air France flight to Paris," Dortmunder said.

Kelp blinked at him. "How'd you do that?"

"Telepathy," Greenwood said. "My stunt is, I guess your weight."

"Let's go up," Dortmunder said.

"I'm not dressed to go up to a place like that," Murch said. He was in a leather jacket and work pants, while the other three were all in suits or sport jackets and ties.

Dortmunder said to Kelp, "Any other way down out of there?"

"Probably. This is the only public way."

"Okay. Murch, you stay down here in case they get through us. If they do, follow them but don't try anything on your own. Kelp, is Chefwick still in the phone booth?"

"No, he said he was going to the O. J. We can leave messages there now."

"Fine. Murch, if somebody comes down and you follow him, leave us a message at the O. J. as soon as you can."

"Right."

The other three rode the escalator upstairs, emerging on a dark carpet in a dark open area. The maître d's lectern, some doweling, and a lot of artificial plants separated this area from the main dining room. The maître d' himself, armed with a French accent less charming than the young lady's at Air France, approached and asked them how many they were. Dortmunder said, "We'll wait for the rest of our party before going in."

"Certainly, sir." The maître d' bowed himself away.

Kelp said, "There they are."

Dortmunder looked through the plastic leaves. The dining room was large, and very nearly empty. At a table in the middle distance, beside a window, sat Major Iko and Prosker and three sturdy young black men. They were having a leisurely dinner, the time now being just a little past five, with over two hours left before their flight.

Kelp said, "I don't like bracing them here. Too public, and too boxed in."

"I agree," Dortmunder said. "All right, we'll wait for them downstairs." He turned and started away.

Greenwood said, "I'll be with you in a minute. Private business."

Dortmunder and Kelp went on ahead, and a minute later Greenwood caught up with them. They filled Murch in, and then the four of them spread out around the waiting room, all keeping their eyes on the escalator to the Golden Door.

It was nearly six o'clock, and afternoon had turned to night outside the terminal's windows when the Major and Prosker and the other three finally came down from dinner. Dortmunder immediately got to his feet and walked toward them. When they saw him, and were still staring in astonishment, he put a big smile on his face, stuck his hand out, and advanced quickly, crying, "Major! What a surprise! It's great to see you again!"

He had reached the group by now, and he grasped the Major's limp hand and started to pump it. Keeping the big smile on his face, he said softly, "The others are all around. If you don't want shooting, just stand still."

Prosker had already been looking around, and now he said, "By God, there they are!"

"Dortmunder," the Major said, "I'm sure we can talk this over."

"You're damn right we can," Dortmunder said. "Just the two of us. No lawyers, no bodyguards."

"You wouldn't get—violent."

"Not me, Major," Dortmunder said. "But I don't know about the others. Greenwood would shoot down Prosker first, that's only natural, but I think Kelp would go first for you."

Prosker said, "You wouldn't dare start anything like that in a crowded place like this."

"Perfect place for it," Dortmunder said. "Shooting. Panic. We mix in with everybody else. Easiest place in the world to hide is in a crowd."

The Major said, "Prosker, don't try to make him prove himself, it has the ring of truth."

"So it does, damn it," said Prosker. "All right, Dortmunder, what do you want? More money?"

"We can't afford a hundred seventy-five thousand," the Major said. "It just wouldn't be possible."

"Two hundred thousand," Dortmunder reminded him. "The price went up back at caper number three. But I don't want to talk in front of all these other people. Come on."

"Come on? Come on where?"

"We're just going to talk," Dortmunder said. "These people can stand here, and my people will stay where they are, and you and me are going over there and talk. Come on."

The Major was very reluctant, but Dortmunder was insistent, and finally the Major started to move. Dortmunder said to the others over his shoulder, "Just stay right here, and you won't start any posthumous panics."

Dortmunder and the Major strolled away down the long corridor overlooking customs, with the duty-free shops on one side of the corridor and on the other side the railing where people can stand and look down at their returning relatives and visiting foreign friends being degraded.

The Major said, "Dortmunder, Talabwo is a poor country. I can get you some more money, but not two hundred thousand dollars. Perhaps fifty thousand, another ten thousand per man. But we just couldn't afford any more."

"So you figured this doublecross from the beginning," Dortmunder said.

"I won't lie to you," the Major said.

Back in the main waiting room, Prosker was saying to the three black men, "If we take off in four different directions, they won't dare shoot."

"We don't want to die," one of the black men said, and the others nodded agreement.

"They won't shoot, damn it!" Prosker insisted. "Don't you know what Dortmunder's up to? He's going to take the emerald away from the Major!"

The black men looked at one another.

"If you don't go help the Major," Prosker said, "and Dortmunder gets that emerald away from him, you'll get worse than shot and you know it."

The black men looked worried.

"I'll count three," Prosker said, "and on three we'll take off in different directions, then all circle around and go down that way after Dortmunder and the Major. I'll go back and to the left, you go straight ahead, you go at an angle to the left that way, and you go right. You all ready?"

They hated it, but the thought of the Major in a bad mood was even worse. Reluctantly they nodded.

"One," Prosker said. He could see Greenwood sitting behind a copy of the *Daily News* way over there. "Two," he said. In another direction he could see Kelp. "Three," he said, and started to run. The black men went on standing there a second or two longer, and then they began to run.

Running people in an airline terminal tend not to be noticed very much, but these four had started so abruptly that a dozen people looked after them in astonishment. Kelp and Greenwood and Murch looked after them too, and then all of a sudden *they* started running, toward one another, for a quick conference.

In the meantime, Dortmunder and the Major were still walking down the corridor, Dortmunder trying to find an unpopulated corner in which to relieve the Major of the emerald and the Major talking on at great length about the poverty of Talabwo, his regret at trying to dupe Dortmunder, and his desire to make amends to the best of his ability.

A distant voice cried, "Dortmunder!" Recognizing it as Kelp's voice, Dortmunder turned and saw two of the black men pelting his way, bouncing customs-oglers left and right.

The Major thought he was going to join the track team, but Dortmunder closed a hand on his elbow and locked it there. He looked around, and just ahead was a closed golden door marked "No Admittance" in black letters. Dortmunder pulled, the door opened, he shoved the Major through and followed him, and there they were at the top of a grimy gray staircase.

The Major said, "Dortmunder, I give you my word—"

"I don't want your word, I want that stone."

"Do you think I'd carry it?"

"That's exactly what you'd do with it, you wouldn't let it out of your sight till you were home free." Dortmunder pulled out Greenwood's revolver and shoved it into the Major's stomach. "It'll take longer if I have to search your body."

"Dortmunder—"

"Shut up and give me the emerald! I don't have time for lies!"

The Major looked in Dortmunder's face, inches from his own, and said, "I'll pay you all the money, I'll—"

"You'll die, damn you! Give me the emerald!"

"All right, all right!" The Major was babbling now, caught up in Dortmunder's urgency. "You hold on to it," he said, pulling the black plush box from his jacket pocket. "There won't be any other buyers. Hold on to it, I'll get in touch with you, I'll find the money to pay you."

Dortmunder snatched the box from his hand, stepped back, opened it and took a quick look inside. The emerald was there. He looked up, and the Major was jumping at him. The Major jumped into the barrel of the gun, and fell backward dazed.

The door opened, and one of the black men started in. Dortmunder hit him in the stomach, remembering that they'd just eaten, and the black man said, "Phooff!" and bent over.

But the other black man was behind him, and the third wouldn't be far away. Dortmunder turned, emerald in one hand and revolver in the other, and raced away down the stairs.

He heard them following him, heard the Major shouting. The first door he came to was locked, and the second one led him outside into the chill darkness of an October evening.

But outside where? Dortmunder stumbled through darkness, rounded a corner, and the night was full of airplanes.

He had gone through the looking glass, past that invisible barrier that closes half the world to unauthorized personnel. He was back where the planes are, in pockets of bright light, surrounded by darkness punctuated by strips of blue lights or amber lights, taxiways, runways, loading zones.

And the black men were still after him. Dortmunder looked to his right, and passengers were disembarking from an SAS plane over there. Join them? Except that he would look a little strange at customs, with no passport, no ticket, no luggage. He turned the other way and there was darkness, and he ran into it.

The next fifteen minutes were hectic ones for Dortmunder. He kept running, and the three black men kept running in his wake. He was all over the territory reserved for airplanes, running now on grass, now on a taxiway, now on gravel, jumping over marker lights, trying not to silhouette himself too clearly against the brightly lit areas and also trying not to get himself run down by a passing 707.

From time to time he saw the civilian part of the airport, his part, the other side of a fence, or around the corner of a building, with people walking and taxis driving along, but every time he headed that way the black men angled to head him off and keep him in the flat open exposed area.

And now he was getting farther and farther away from buildings, bright lights, all connection with the passengers' part of the terminal. The runways were dead ahead, with the long lines of planes waiting their turns to take off. An Olympia jet would take off, followed by a Mohawk twin-engine prop plane, followed by a pop singer's Lear jet, followed by an ancient two-seater Ercoupe, followed by a Lufthansa 707, the monsters and the midgets one after another, obediently taking their turns, the big guys never shouldering the little guys out of the way, that being done for them in the control tower.

One of the planes waiting to take off was a Waco Vela, an Italian-built, American-assembled single-engine five-seater with an American-made Franklin engine. At the controls was a computer salesman named Firgus, with his friend Bullock asleep across the back seat. Ahead of him was a TWA jet, which trundled into place at the head of the runway, roared and vibrated a few seconds, and then began galumphing away like Sidney Greenstreet playing basketball. Till it became airborne, at which point it also became graceful and beautiful.

Firgus drove his little plane forward, out onto the runway, and turned right. Now the runway stretched ahead of him. Firgus sat there looking at his controls, waiting for the tower to give him the go-ahead, and regretting the chop suey he'd had for dinner, and all at once the right-hand door opened and a man with a gun got in.

Firgus stared at him in astonishment. "Havana?" he said.

"Just up in the sky will do," Dortmunder told him and looked out the side window at the three black men running his way.

"Okay, N733W," the tower said in Firgus's earphones. "Cleared for takeoff."

"Uh," said Firgus.

Dortmunder looked at him. "Don't do anything stupid," he said. "Just take off."

"Yes," Firgus said. Luckily he was an old hand with this plane and could fly it while his mind was doing flip-flops. He set the Vela going, they skeetered away down the runway, the black men came to a panting stop way back there, and the Vela climbed abruptly into the air.

"Good," Dortmunder said.

Firgus looked at him. "If you shoot me," he said, "we'll crash and you'll die too."

"I won't shoot anybody," Dortmunder said.

"But we can't make it to Cuba," Firgus said. "With

the gas I've got, we wouldn't make it much past Washington."

"I don't want to go to Cuba," Dortmunder said. "I don't want to go to Washington either."

"Then where do you want to go? Not over the ocean, that's even longer."

"Where were you going?"

Firgus couldn't figure any of this out. "Well," he said, "Pittsburgh, actually."

"Head that way," Dortmunder said.

"You want to go to Pittsburgh?"

"Just do what you were going to do," Dortmunder said. "Don't mind me."

"Well," Firgus said. "All right."

Dortmunder looked at the sleeping man in back, then out the window at the lights going by in the darkness below. They were away from the airport already. The Balabomo Emerald was in Dortmunder's jacket pocket. Things were more or less under control.

It took fifteen minutes to fly over New York and reach New Jersey, and Firgus was silent all that time. But he seemed to relax a little more when they were over the darker, quieter New Jersey swamp, and he said, "Boy, I don't know what your problem is, but you sure scared the dickens out of me."

"Sorry," Dortmunder said. "I was in a hurry."

"I guess you must have been." Firgus glanced around at Bullock, who was still asleep. "Does *he* have a surprise coming," he said.

But Bullock kept on sleeping, and another quarter

hour went by, and then Dortmunder said, "What's that down there?"

"What's what?"

"That sort of pale strip."

Firgus looked down and said, "Oh, that's Route Eighty. You know, one of the new superhighways they're building. That part isn't done yet. And they're obsolete, you know. This is the coming thing, the small private plane. Why, do you know—"

"It looks done," Dortmunder said.

"What?"

"That road down there. It looks done."

"Well, it isn't open yet." Firgus was irritated. He wanted to tell Dortmunder the wonderful statistics of private plane ownership in the United States.

"Land there," Dortmunder said.

Firgus stared at him. "Do what?"

"It's wide enough for a plane like this," Dortmunder said. "Land there."

"Why?"

"So I can get out. Don't worry, I'm still not going to shoot you."

Firgus banked the plane and circled back over the pale strip on the dark ground below. "I don't know," he said dubiously. "There's no lights or anything."

"You can do it," Dortmunder told him. "You're a good pilot, I can tell you are." He didn't know anything about flying at all.

Firgus preened. "Well, I suppose I could bring her in down there," he said. "Be a little tricky, but not impossible."

"Good."

Firgus circled twice more before making the attempt. He was clearly nervous, and his nervousness communicated itself to Dortmunder, who almost told him to fly on, they'd find someplace better farther on. But there wouldn't be anyplace better. Dortmunder couldn't have Firgus land at a regular airport anywhere, so it had to be something irregular, and at least that was a straight ribbon of concrete down there, and wide enough to land the plane on.

Which Firgus did, very well, once he'd built his nerve up to it. He landed as light as a feather, brought the Vela to a stop in seven hundred feet, and turned a huge smile at Dortmunder. "That's what I call flying," he said.

"Me too," Dortmunder said.

Firgus looked at Bullock again and said testily, "I wish to hell he'd wake up." He poked Bullock's shoulder. "Wake up!"

"Let him alone," Dortmunder said.

"If he doesn't see you," Firgus said, "he won't believe any of this. Hey, Bullock! God damn it, man, you're missing an adventure!" He punched Bullock's shoulder again, a little harder than before.

"Thanks for the lift," Dortmunder said and got out of the plane.

"Bullock!" shouted Firgus, pummeling and punching his friend. "Will you for Christ's sake wake up!"

Dortmunder walked away into the darkness.

Bullock came up to consciousness amid a rain of blows, sat up, yawned, rubbed his face, looked around, blinked, frowned, and said, "Where the hell are we?"

"Route Eighty in Jersey," Firgus told him. "Look, do you see that guy? Look quick, will you, before he's out of sight!"

"Route Eighty? We're in an airplane, Firgus!"

"Will you *look*!"

"What the hell you doin' on the *ground*? You want to cause an accident? What are you doin' on Route Eighty?"

"He's out of sight," Firgus said, throwing up his hands in disgust. "I asked you to look, but no."

"You must be drunk, or somethin'," Bullock said. "You're driving an *airplane* down Route Eighty!"

"I'm not driving an airplane down Route Eighty!"

"Well, what the hell do you call it then?"

"We were hijacked, God damn it! A guy jumped on the plane with a gun and—"

"You should of been in the air, it wouldn't of happened."

"Back at Kennedy! Just before we took off, he jumped in with a gun and hijacked us."

"Oh, sure he did," Bullock said. "And here we are in lovely Havana."

"He didn't want to go to Havana."

"No. He wanted to go to New Jersey. He hijacked an airplane to take him to New Jersey."

"Can I help it?" yelled Firgus. "It's what happened!"

"One of us is having a bad dream," Bullock said, "and since you're at the wheel I hope it's me."

"If you'd woke up in time—"

"Yeah, well, wake me when we get to the Delaware Water Gap. I don't want to miss the expression on their faces when an airplane drives up to the tollbooth." Bullock shook his head and lay down again.

Firgus stayed half turned in the seat, glowering at him. "A guy hijacked us," he said, voice dangerously soft. "It did happen."

"If you're gonna fly this low," Bullock said, with his eyes closed, "why not stop at a diner and get us a couple coffees and Danish to go."

"When we get to Pittsburgh," Firgus said, "I am going to punch you in the mouth." And he faced front, turned the Vela around, took off, and flew in a bright fury all the way to Pittsburgh.

6

The Akinzi Ambassador to the United Nations was a large stout man named Nkolimi. One rainy October afternoon, Ambassador Nkolimi was sitting in his private dining room in the Akinzi embassy, a narrow townhouse on East 63rd Street in Manhattan, when a member of the staff came in and said, "Ambassador, there is a man outside who wants to see you."

The Ambassador was eating a Sara Lee Cinnamon Nut Coffee Cake at the moment. The whole thing, all by himself, which was one of the reasons he was such a very stout man. It was his midafternoon snack for today. He was drinking with it coffee with cream and sugar. He was enjoying himself hugely, in more than one meaning of the term, and he disliked being interrupted. He said, "What does he want to see me about?"

"He says it concerns the Balabomo Emerald."

The Ambassador frowned. "He's a policeman?"

"I don't think so, Ambassador."

"What do you think he is?"

"A gangster, Ambassador."

The Ambassador lifted an eyebrow. "Really," he said. "Bring him here, this gangster."

"Yes, Ambassador."

The staff member went away, and the Ambassador filled the waiting time and his mouth with Sara Lee Cinnamon Nut Coffee Cake. He was just adding coffee when the staff member returned and said, "I have him here, sir."

The Ambassador waved a hand to have the gangster brought in, and Dortmunder was ushered into his presence. The Ambassador motioned for Dortmunder to sit down across the table, and Dortmunder did so. The Ambassador, still chewing and swallowing, made hand motions suggestive of offering some coffee cake to Dortmunder, but Dortmunder said, "No, thank you." The Ambassador drank some more coffee, swallowed hugely, patted his lips with his napkin, and said, "Ahh. Now. I understand you want to talk about the Balabomo Emerald."

"That's right," Dortmunder said.

"What do you want to say about it?"

"In the first place," Dortmunder said, "this is just between you and me. No police."

"Well, they're looking for it, of course."

"Sure." Dortmunder looked at the staff member, standing alertly near the door, and back at the Ambassador. "I don't like saying things in front of two witnesses, that's all," he said.

The Ambassador smiled and shook his head. "You'll

have to chance it, I'm afraid," he said. "I prefer not to be alone with strangers."

Dortmunder thought about it for a few seconds, then said, "All right. A little over four months ago, somebody stole the Balabomo Emerald."

"I know that," said the Ambassador.

"It's very valuable," Dortmunder said.

The Ambassador nodded. "I know that too," he said. "Are you building up to an offer to sell it back to me?"

"Not exactly," said Dortmunder. "Most valuable stones," he said, "have imitations made up by their owners, to put on display here and there. Are there any imitations of the Balabomo Emerald?"

"Several," said the Ambassador. "And I dearly wish one of them had been on display at the Coliseum."

Dortmunder glanced mistrustfully at the staff member, then said, "I'm here to offer a trade."

"A trade?"

"The real emerald for one of the imitations."

The Ambassador waited for Dortmunder to go on, then said with a puzzled smile, "I'm afraid I don't understand. The imitation, and what else?"

"Nothing else," Dortmunder said. "A straight trade, one stone for the other."

"I don't follow that," the Ambassador admitted.

"Oh, and one thing more," Dortmunder said. "You don't make any public announcement that you've got it back until I give you the all-clear. Maybe a year or two, maybe less."

The Ambassador pursed his lips. "It seems to me," he said, "you have a fascinating story to tell."

"Not in front of two witnesses," said Dortmunder.

"Very well," said the Ambassador and turned to his staff member. "Wait out in the hall," he said.

"Yes, Ambassador."

When they were alone, the Ambassador said, "Now."

"Here's what happened," Dortmunder said, and told him the whole story, without names, except for Major Iko's. The Ambassador listened, nodding from time to time, smiling from time to time, tut-tutting from time to time, and when Dortmunder was done he said, "Well. I suspected the Major might have something to do with the theft. All right, he tried to cheat you and you got the emerald back. Now what?"

"Someday," Dortmunder said, "the Major's going to come back with two hundred thousand dollars. It might be next month, next year, I don't know when, but I know it'll happen. He really wants that emerald."

"Talabwo does, yes," the Ambassador said.

"So they'll raise the cash," Dortmunder said. "The last thing the Major shouted after me was that I should hold on to the emerald, he'd come pay me, and I know he will."

"But you don't want to give him the emerald any more, is that it? Because he cheated you."

"Right. What I want to give him now is the business. And I will. That's why I want to work this trade. You get the real emerald, and keep it under wraps for a while. I take the imitation and hold on to it till the Major shows up. Then I sell it to him for two hundred thousand bucks, he takes it home to Africa on the plane, you break the story about having the real emerald back."

The Ambassador gave a rueful smile. "They would not treat the Major well in Talabwo," he said, "if he paid two hundred thousand dollars for a piece of green glass."

"That's what I kind of thought."

Still smiling, the Ambassador shook his head and said, "I must make a memo to myself never to try to cheat you."

Dortmunder said, "Is it a deal?"

"Of course it's a deal," said the Ambassador. "Aside from having the emerald back, aside from anything else at all, it's a deal because I've waited years to give the Major one in the eye. I could tell some stories of my own, you know. Are you sure you won't have some coffee cake?"

"Maybe just a little slice," Dortmunder said.

"And some coffee. I insist." The Ambassador glanced over at the rain-smeared window. "Isn't it a beautiful day," he said.

"Beautiful," said Dortmunder.